Highland

Shapeshifter

Clover Autrey

This is a work of fiction. Names, characters, places, and incidents are either the product of the author's imagination or are used fictitiously, and any resemblance to actual persons living or dead, business establishments, events, or locales, is entirely coincidental.

Published by Red Rover Books
Cover art by Pat Autrey
Photos used to design cover were legally obtained from Dreamstime.com

Copyright © 2012 Clover Autrey

All rights reserved.

ISBN- **148017761X**

ISBN-13: **978-1480177611**

HIGHLAND SORCERY NOVELS

HIGHLAND SORCERER
THE VAMPIRE AND THE HIGHLAND EMPATH
HIGHLAND SHAPESHIFTER
HIGHLAND MOON SIFTER

THE ANOINTED

DEMON TRACKERS
BANSHEE'S CRY
A HAUNTING

THE EAGLEKIN SERIES

UPON EAGLE'S LIGHT
CHASE THE WIND
FALLEN WARRIOR

OTHER BOOKS BY CLOVER AUTREY

SEA BORN
THE SWEETHEART TREE

To Pat and the boys for letting me drag them to the Scottish Festival and Highland Games on a hot, windy Saturday in Texas.

My wonderful CPs, the Cowtown Critiquers, for our great brain-storming sessions, even when we don't get anything done. I love your creative energy.

And to my fabulous editor, Melodee "Mac" Curtis. You are the best and I love you.

Hugs to you all.

Highland Shapeshifter

Seattle, Washington, Present Day

Ogres stink.

There's no getting around the odor. Even with the astringent scent of white spearmint oil Lenore had dabbed beneath her nose, the bar reeked. She'd probably have to burn these clothes.

High tones from an elfish lyre lilted out from the scratchy speaker system, an airy enchantment squashed instantly by the musty dark atmosphere of the pub.

"In back." Gainy, Starch's right hand man, well, ogre, canted his bulbous head, displacing swirls of smoke with the movement. "Been waiting on you, Little Pix."

Lenore rolled her eyes and tucked the wayward strands of her white-blond bangs back beneath her knitted cap. "I bet he has. The shipment came early then?"

"Not exactly. Starch has something better."

"What?" Lenore whirled on the fidgety ogre, her head barely topping near his protruding ribcage. She jabbed a finger at him. She needed this shipment. Like yesterday. The vamps wouldn't be able to hold off the blood addiction without the *crimson tear* and she didn't even want to think about how the Ifrits had been managing to keep from randomly combusting into cinders without larkspur this long. She was surprised fires hadn't been breaking out throughout the city

She'd left in the middle of the night at Starch's first call, prepared with more than extra in payment to get her hands on the underground supplies.

"What the hell is this, Gainy? I don't need something better. I need what I arranged for." See, she could swear and act all tough when she had to, and in this environment, she had to. Lenore sidestepped between big bad Gainy and a ghoul who was exhaling blue smoke through a clear straw, shoved up a piggish snout. In her dealings with the ogres, she'd learned to not let them play her. Be decisive and only leave with what she asked for. And pay in cash. For all their gruff and burly natures, they were the slickest salesmen on the planet and she didn't want to owe them. Don Corleone had nothing on Starch.

Horse's head, phew. Try waking up to the severed head of a phooka in your bed. Of course, that had never happened to her because she always played it straight with the godfather of warts and slime. But she'd heard...

"Tell Starch to contact me when my stuff gets here. He knows I don't want anything to do with his other dealings."

Gainy grabbed her arm, stopping her. "Oh, you'll want to see this."

Lenore glanced at the meaty brown hand encircling her entire upper arm, before pointedly glaring straight up into Gainy's triple-pupiled eyes. She had a can of wasp spray in her messenger bag, hanging by her hip, but doubted she'd need it with him. Intimidation worked just fine. She narrowed her eyes, going for the toughest facial expression she could muster. Okay, yeah, she knew she didn't have the build for threatening anyone twice her size, let alone an ogre, but she could bluff.

He immediately let go, lifting his palms outward in the sign of surrender. They stared in a non-verbal stand-off, while the graceful notes of the lyre flowed around them.

Gainy blinked first, and Lenore felt a smug moment of triumph until his warty lip twitched. "It involves your sister."

Everything went cold. And hard.

In a flash, her fists were bunched in Gainy's collar and she'd pulled his fat head down to her level. "My sister has nothing to do with our arrangements," she hissed in his face. All the occupants in the bar went quiet. That anger was not a bluff.

Lenore kept Charity in the dark. Her sister had no idea where Lenore got the more hard-to-get ingredients for their herbal shop. She'd be furious if she ever found out about the risks Lenore had been taking. After laughing her butt off that her little sister who'd rather be in a library surrounded by books was getting away with it.

"Easy." Gainy pried her hands away.

He was a lackey anyway. Fists balled, Lenore strode to the back room, and yanked open the door.

Starch had his broad lumpy back to her, taking inventory of whatever was in several large crates on the scuffed work table. He turned toward her, the protruding hairless brow bone lifted above his too-small reading glasses. "Ah, Little Pixie, excellent timing."

She wasn't in a tolerant mood. "I thought we were friends." Okay, that was pushing it. "Yet you have Gainy threatening my sister?"

"I did no such thing." Starch had the audacity to look put upon. His gaze swept beyond her shoulder where Gainy had come into the storeroom behind her.

Lenore shifted to the side to keep both ogres in sight.

Starch put down the clipboard he'd been marking inventory on. "If anything, I'm looking out for you and your sister. Got a shipment in I think you'll find interesting."

She tilted her head. "I'm listening." Her instincts

screamed *get out, get out now.* Something was terribly off, but she couldn't back down, not if she wanted to find out what was going on.

Starch snorted. "Suspicious little healer, aren't we?"

She responded with a raised finger, reeling inside. She'd never flipped anyone off in her life. This faux life of crime was really hauling her out of her comfort zone.

The ogre cackled in throaty glee. "Come on, then. It's back here."

She followed him to the rear of the storeroom, pushing past stacked crates and covered bundles that Starch had to squeeze his bulk sideways between. Gainy came up behind them.

He brought her to a lumpy tarp on the floor, wedged up between a rickety shelf and the building's water pipe that ran from floor to ceiling.

"So where is it?" she asked and something beneath the tarp moved at the sound of her voice.

Lenore flinched back. Dang it. So much for being too tough to react to a little movement. Covering, she whirled on the ogres. "What is that?" She knew Starch's business stretched into unsavory areas, but, as yet, she'd never seen any evidence that he was blatantly involved in the trafficking of magical and mythical creatures.

Her heart slammed against her rib cage. Backing away, she shook her head. Playing the bad chick to help otherworldly folk was one thing, but getting involved in anything seedier... Nope, she wasn't going to go there. "I'm out."

The creature, whatever it was beneath the tarp, jerked again, followed by a quiet moan that shot straight to her gut.

"No one's stopping you," Starch said. His round eyes blinked. He knew he had her.

Damn her healer's heart. It was the sole reason she did business with Starch in the first place. To get the supplies necessary to help magic wielders who couldn't get help anywhere else. Another curse word slipped out quite naturally to her subconscious. She was on a roll.

She needed to know what all this had to do with Charity.

Resolved, she edged forward and dragged the heavy tarp off the creature underneath.

And stared.

It was just a man.

He sat against the sewage pipe, arms pulled behind him, either tied or handcuffed. His head hung forward, dark hair obscuring his face. His jeans were ripped and loose, as was his dirty T-shirt, splattered with blood and mud. Cuts and abrasions speckled his arms and she'd guess there were more under his shirt and on his face. Anger at his harsh mistreatment rose up in her.

"You're into trafficking humans now?"

"Ha!" Starch flung his large hands up. "Hardly human.

Shapeshifter. And a powerful one at that. Took three ghouls and a troll to subdue him and that was after they tranqed him."

"Is he still drugged?" She crouched down beside the guy, squeezing her hands into fists to hide the anger. This wasn't right. "What'd you give him?"

She touched his arm and he flinched. Her heart went out to him. He looked young and innocent. A year or so younger than her, maybe eighteen or nineteen. Too young to be caught up in whatever mess this was. Her instinct was to soothe, but she couldn't show any softness here. Grabbing his chin, she lifted his head.

And the world narrowed down to a pair of mossy green eyes.

Energy shot into her, buzzing strangely across her skin in a lightning rapid pulse. An instant familiarity burned through her, as if she knew him, though she was certain she'd never seen him before, but there was something. Staring into his battered face, a connection rippled between them, tangent and swift and then was gone as quickly as it came.

Stranger still, she wanted that connection back.

Lenore blinked.

The telltale sign of drugs dilated his pupils.

She swallowed, shaking off the odd feeling. "I asked what you gave him."

"Tanglewort."

She inwardly winced. Geez, if he tried to shift with that in his system...

"How much and when was his last dose?" She glared at the ogres.

"Less than an hour ago. Seven cc's." Gainy shuffled from foot to foot. Lenore quickly calculated. It usually took at least nine hours for tanglewort to clear a person's system, a little less if the user was large and though he appeared lean, this guy was plenty big.

"Don't get all pissy with me," Starch growled. "I'm doing you a favor. Him here was out in Portland, sniffing around about a Charity Greves of Seattle."

Lenore stiffened at that, listening intently as she looked over the poor guy for bruises or any cuts large enough they'd need to be taken care of right away. Not that she wanted to use any healing magic in front of the ogres and make herself vulnerable.

"One of my guys caught wind of it." Starch didn't filter the smugness from his voice. "So I had them bottle him up and ship him out here. Figured you didn't need the trouble of any unsavories asking about your innocent sister."

No, she definitely did not. "Because you're a true humanitarian. You couldn't have asked him to come along nicely? Geez, Starch, he's just a kid."

"A kid with teeth, so as it turns out, no. Seemed the *kid* didn't like our terms. Shifted into a real wild cat. Literally."

Not to mention there'd be nothing in it for Starch.

She stood and craned her neck way up to face the ogre. "Okay. So what do you want?"

"Three Gs. Up front tonight and you can have him. Another two in the morning."

"Five thousand?"

"I know of three other buyers right now who will give me twice that for a shifter of his caliber. He's not only powerful, but pretty. A real lucrative combination."

"Then you shouldn't have hit his face."

"Like I said, he didn't come easily and as I also said, I'm doing you a favor. Are you hard of hearing all of a sudden? You interested or not?"

Ah man. There was no way the guy could take much more tanglewort and not shift. He couldn't take being with Starch much longer. He'd feel an irrational need to shift and when he did, under the drug's influence, he'd have no control over the transformation. Best case scenario, he'd shift into something harmless. Worst case, he'd fall into the moment between shifts when he was pure energy and simply dissipate himself right out of existence.

"You know I wouldn't walk in here with that kind of cash on me." She'd brought two thousand dollars for the supplies, more than enough. "One thousand now and three in the morning. I have it stashed, don't even need to do a bank run."

Starch's nostrils twitched. He was greedy, but in his

line of work, cash on the table always outweighed a future promise of a sale.

"Fifteen hundred now," he countered.

Gainy's front pocket lit up. The burr of a cell phone vibrated.

"Fine. Deal." Lenore held out her hand.

"Uh, boss." The thin cell phone looked incongruous against Gainy's fleshy ear. "Another interested party just showed. Lan's got them out front."

"Really?" Starch swiveled in the small space, clearly surprised. "What's the offer?"

Gainy turned away, speaking into the phone.

Lenore glanced back at the man. She couldn't let this happen. "Hold up a minute. We have a deal."

"Not yet." Distracted, Starch watched Gainy.

The ogre held his hand over the phone. "He says triple what anyone else will offer."

"Triple?" What could only be described as delight lit Starch's features. "Tell Lan to bring them back."

"Wait, no. Starch, you can't."

"That's the beauty of it. I can."

"I raise my offer." This would deplete her emergency funds.

Starch was already squeezing back out between the crates. "Yes, do that. That will make the buyer up his price. A bidding war. Come along."

"No, Starch. My sister…"

He stopped and looked back, brow bones lowered. "Here's what I'll do. For one G, I'll give you an hour to get answers out of him. I'll even have my guys work him over to make it easier for you." His lips spread in a parody of a smile meant to placate.

Seriously? Dread knotted her belly, even as she felt herself nod. "One hour."

"Done."

Starch inclined his head and walked past the crates into the open area of the storeroom where Gainy waited.

Lenore leaned against one of the crates, suddenly shaky, her mind running through scenarios of wealthy buyers dragging the shapeshifter off to do who knows what with him. Geez, why should she even care? He was nothing to her. She didn't even know for sure what the other buyers wanted with him. Maybe it wouldn't be so bad. She internally rolled her eyes at how bad she was at trying to rationalize and looked back to where the shifter slumped against the bonds on his arms, her heart squeezing at that sudden flash of whatever it was that had passed between them. She couldn't do it. She couldn't just get her answers and walk away.

Damn it to hell. That sentiment spilled out without any coaxing. Look at her mouthy mind go.

She swallowed. This was going to cost her. If not her entire savings, then in her underground supply contacts. Too bad, she actually kind of liked Starch and he always came through with the rare supplies.

She moved to the end of the crates to see who her competitors for the shifter were. The door from the main bar room swung inward and another ogre, Starch's bouncer Lan—like a bar full of ogres needed a specified bouncer—ducked through, followed by two men and a woman.

They wore expensive leather and jeans, each young and attractive. They looked like a yuppie biker group, out to buy an exotic shapeshifter with daddy's money. She instantly disliked them, not to mention if their attire was anything to go by, they could outbid her a hundred times over.

"We want him," one of the men got right to it.

"Slow down," Starch said. "I like new acquaintances. I'm a friendly sort after all, but first we need to verify the color of your money. And none of those Canadian monopoly bills."

Lenore eased back between the crates, and slid to her knees beside the shifter.

She touched his arm and again that current of electricity jolted between them.

His head snapped up and he tried to focus on her with red-rimmed eyes beneath long sweaty bangs.

"Shh, easy. I'm going to get you out of here." She pressed him forward to look at how he was bound. His wrists were clamped together behind the pipe with a plastic zip tie instead of cuffs or rope. Good. Easy peasy.

She pulled her pocket knife from inside her boot and clicked it open.

A thud banged loudly. A pulse of energy ripped across Lenore's flesh, raising the tiny hairs on her arms. Some freakish sort of blue light flashed across the ceiling. The crates rocked, one tipping and crashed with a cloud of dust lifting off the floor.

What was that?

She slashed through the zip tie, releasing the guy.

Shouts and growls echoed through the store room, followed by staccato bangs. That sound she recognized. Gunfire. Starch must not have liked the yuppie buyers' offer.

In a motion more fluid than his drugged state should have allowed, the shifter was on his feet. Light shimmered across his skin in a build-up of magic.

"Hey!" Lenore swung around to his front and jabbed a finger up in his face. He was taller than she'd expected. "You're doped up! No shifting."

Blurry eyes blinked down at her. She couldn't tell if he was coherent enough to understand until finally he nodded and the shimmer around him dimmed.

Gainy sailed back into the crates. Wood and glass flew everywhere, boxes spilling across the floor. More shots rang out. Resilient, the ogre shook it off and rushed back into the fray.

Lenore grabbed the shifter's wrist. "We got to get out of here." She glanced around. She'd never been back this far in the storeroom before.

"He's here!" One of the yuppies, a blond guy, came around a tarped crate. He was carrying some weird kind of wide-butted gun.

"Not that way." Scrabbling at the shifter's shirt, her fingers catching in the tears already there, she pulled, dodging behind more crates. The material of his shirt ripped, even as he kept close behind her.

Shots whined around them, ricocheting off the cinder-block walls and impacting wood. The blue glowing streaks whirled in the air. Whatever the yuppies wanted the shifter for they weren't concerned about leaving holes in him. Then again, the ray guns hadn't opened up any of the ogres either.

They came to a dead-end, cornered between walls and heavy shelves. They spun at the quiet snick of a boot on cement.

The second yuppie guy with dark hair had them in his cross-sights. At least the gun he carried was a regular handgun. And who knew if that was a good or bad thing? The other came at them, shoving a box out of his way. Where had the woman gotten off to? The shifter edged to the side, putting himself between her and the gun's muzzle.

"All right now," Yuppie Ken Doll said. "Don't move."

His lip curled at the same instant he flew into the wall, body-checked by a raging bulldozer of Starch.

"You think you can come into my pl—"

The blond yuppie jerked his weapon toward the ogre and the shifter pounced into action, running straight into the guy, flipping him off his feet and kept on going.

Lenore stared after his retreating backside wide-eyed. Well, he was gone. She'd never see his hide again, not that she blamed him.

Crashes banged up front. Gainy and the woman?

Starch lifted the guy he had body-slammed off the floor. The guy moaned. Lenore would not want to be him. Starch's eyes bulged.

"Wanna run by me again how you're just gonna take my property?"

Lenore edged around them. Time to play scarce while she was still in one piece.

"No." A feminine voice barked. She came face-to-muzzle with the business end of the really strange looking gun. Up close and way too personal, it looked more like something out of a video game. The yuppie woman's eyes narrowed. "Where's the shifter?" The gun hummed, ramping up to recharge for another blast of blue. Yep, definitely a weapon straight out of the comics. Must be some homemade tech junkie's dream.

Lenore eased her head sideways out of the line of fire. "Did what shifters do best. Tucked tail and ran."

The woman frowned. Her eyes tracked toward the ogre pounding the snot out of her friend.

"You gonna deal with that?" Lenore lifted her hands. "'Cause I'm not in this."

The woman's gun shifted back toward her. "Oh, you're in this."

She had short blond hair, almost silver blond, with long side-swept bangs, which she flipped out of her eyes with a toss of her head.

"Bekah!" The yuppie guy sailed through the air, arms and legs flailing, and landed in a jarring heap.

"Dammit." The woman shot at Starch, a streak of blue light and whirring purr that pushed the ogre back into a pile of crates. Okay, so the ray gun did pack enough of a punch to throw a two-ton ogre like that. She'd be impressed if she wasn't so stunned. The following concussion of force vibrated through the floor.

Whoa. What a kick. Nearly rocked off her feet, Lenore took that as her cue to high-tail it. She ducked between swaying crates, narrowly escaping as they crashed behind her. Score one for being small. Packets of orange crystals broke across the floor, lifting in clouds of noxious powder. She hoped it wasn't anything toxic, quickly covering her face and trying not to breathe it in, and slammed into a wall of ogre.

"Hey!" Lan's meaty fists grabbed her, swallowing most of her upper arms between his fingers. The ogre bouncer was on his knees, huge eyes dazed and way too heavy, dragging her down as he tried to use her as support. Apparently whatever those blue streaks the yuppies shot could only immobilize ogres for so long.

"Lan, let go. Starch is back there. He needs your help!" She tried to shrug out of his grasp, but he was still too out of it and pushing down on her as an aide to make it to his own lumbering feet. His bulk was crushing her. "Lan!"

"The lass said tae let go."

Both their heads snapped up.

The shapeshifter leapt out of nowhere, taking them all to the floor. Lenore hit the ogre's belly hard and was immediately dragged up around the waist and set on her feet. The shifter's head canted, looking her over.

"Stop!" The yuppie woman called out and that whining build-up of her weapon purred out. The shifter yanked Lenore between another row of crates as blue light exploded beside them, the concussion of it rocking through the air.

Hand in hand, they ran. Shouts and thuds poured after them.

"Do you know where you're going?" Lenore shouted.

The guy twisted to look back at her. Dark brows pulled together like a shrug. "Away from the noise. I thought that would be best."

Of course. Geez, why didn't she think of that? Poor

guy was still completely out of it. Yet even drugged to the gills...Lenore's heart squeezed a little...he'd come back for her.

Another pulse of light whined close. The guy's hand tugged on hers.

"Let me lead." She squeezed past him, not letting go and pulled him along. There had to be a rear door. Starch would never let himself be boxed in without an escape in his own place, but so far she hadn't seen any windows or doors beyond the stacks and stacks of boxes.

She really didn't want to head back through—wait, were those stairs? Veering that way, Lenore tried to see beyond a tall partly covered gilded picture frame to where a set of rusted metal steps led. There was a single door high up in the cinderblock wall. The steps and door didn't look wide enough to support an ogre's frame though, but you never knew. Starch was good at taking care of Starch. Was it a dead end?

The shifter followed her right up to the steps, his glassy gaze wary. "Ye're certain?"

She winced, thinking the same thing he must be, that the stairs would expose them to the yuppies' ray gun darts of fury.

"No. Not really."

The grin he turned on her was drop-dead brain-cell-killing sexy. He didn't look quite as young and innocent as before.

"Up ye go, then, lass." Not wasting another second, he practically lifted her onto the third step and clamored up behind her, placing his own back in the direct line of fire.

"Bekah, Matthew," one of the yuppies called out. White-laced preppy names if she ever heard any. "Stairs."

Crap. They'd never make it. The whine of their mail order kit alien weapons built up.

Starch was suddenly there, looking up at them from the bottom of the steps, all three of his large pupils rimmed in silver. That was a new twist on adrenaline, she noted for future reference if she ever decided to study ogre anatomy. Yep, that was the curse and the gift of her mind, always storing random information like a walking breathing index file. But if you couldn't learn something new while fleeing for your life, what good were you? "Four thousand. Final offer."

"Deal. You got it." Lenore shouted, ready to throw out her cash right then.

"What I do for you," the ogre growled and threw himself up onto the metal grating of the stairs like an acrobat, shaking the groaning steps, his huge girth covering them as the blue light speared his chest and every muscle in his body went stiff as a board. He teetered forward on the successive buffet of air and fell forward, hitting the floor, smashing crates in a flume of dust.

Stunned, Lenore stared over the shifter's shoulder until he nudged her upward.

The weapons purred again, powering up for a second wave.

"Go," Shifter Dude hissed behind her. She was already taking two steps at a time. They made it to the door without being shot at. Lenore yanked the knob and it didn't budge.

Seriously?

She rattled it, trying to open the stupid door. The two weird guns whined louder.

The shifter reached across her waist, covered her hand and calmly twisted the knob. It released with a click. He smiled sweetly, lifting his chin forward to indicate she should go through it.

Oh. So he had a bit of a smart ass in him.

Together they shoved open the door, spilling out into a back alley. He quickly slammed the door closed as blue light shot between the door's edges.

"C'mon." Lenore sped off, stopping when the guy wasn't immediately following. "Come on."

He leaned against the door, shaking his head dazedly before pushing off and immediately blanched, swaying.

Lenore ran to him, pressing up beneath his arm. "Whoa, hey there. Sorry, I forgot about the drugs." It was a wonder he'd managed this far.

"Drugs?" His brows rose in confusion, giving him a lost puppy quality.

She smiled. "Let's just get out of here for now before

our friends burst through that door. Think you can walk?"

He nodded, seemingly too out of energy to speak and took a step forward, which almost pitched him to the ground.

Lenore took most of his weight, managing to keep them both from face-planting. Barely. "That'd be a no on walking. New plan. Just stay upright and I'll do the rest."

Chapter Two

She nearly got him to her car parked around the front of Starch's bar before the shifter's legs gave out. Dang tanglewort was beginning to wreak havoc with his coordination.

"Whoa, okay, gotcha big guy."

His weight almost bowled her over. "My car's right here. Think you can make two more steps?"

Squinting, he gave her a sloppy smile, which fell when his gaze landed on her little red Prius. Yeah, she wondered how he was going to fold into the thing too.

Pressing tight into his chest to keep him on his feet, she reached over and wrestled the door open.

"Stay," she ordered and eased away a little so she could get the passenger seat moved back. He had the presence of mind to grab hold of the top of the car and the door to keep upright and nodded for her that he wasn't going to fall.

Between his body and the car Lenore felt rather puny. Masculine strength radiated off him. What in the world was she going to do with him? He wasn't a sweet kid a year younger than her, but a man, dangerous and big. Probably unsafe to be around. Starch had thought so at any rate, enough to keep the merchandize incoherent. He didn't seem so dangerous now, but that didn't mean he couldn't be. He was a shifter losing every bit of his sense of control to drugs. Of course that was dangerous.

Chills skittered across her scalp. Better he was with her than an innocent bystander on the streets if he lost it. Even without needing to know what he was asking around about her sister for, she couldn't have left him to whatever those gun-toting yuppies had in mind for him.

She got the seat pushed back and turned, nearly colliding with his chin. He'd begun to sag, his arms shaking on the car and open door. They were pressed so close she saw small flecks of darker green in his light eyes. Doors slammed farther down the alleyway.

Poor guy looked as though he was about to drop.

"We are traveling in this wee *car*?" He said *car* like it was a new word he was still testing. His lips curled lazily. "I like *cars*."

"Well, it's the only one I got. Come on." Scooping herself beneath his arms, she guided him around to back into the seat. He was all gangly uncoordinated limbs, trying to fit into the seat while he smiled crookedly at her with adoring eyes. He looked sweet, not like some threatening imposing shapeshifter.

She pretty much shoved him in, closing the door on his large frame and raced to the other side.

Shouts chased after her. *Come on come on come on*. She dug her keys out, fumbling them into the ignition.

"Stop!" the blond Malibu Ken yuppie shouted.

Lenore hit the gas as he filled her rear view mirror and she sped away.

The shifter flopped over, dark head pushing against her arm. "This *car* is tiny. As are you."

Her heart plowed ahead a mile a minute.

"Hey." She bumped her arm up, trying to shift the guy back into his own seat but he was out, the drugs clearly taking their toll.

Lenore drove deeper into the city, away from her apartment. She couldn't take him there. Not that she thought Starch would tell the yuppies where she lived after how they tried to cheat him, but she wouldn't trust the ogre not to be bought if the price was satisfactory either.

There was only one place to go and she seriously did not want to go there.

Wincing, she dug her cell out of her pocket, awkwardly steering with the cutie pie's forehead ground into her shoulder and punched the number.

It took six rings before he picked up, all groggy voiced from sleep. "Mmmmmph."

"I need you to open your garage."

Silence coated the other end as it sank in who was calling him this time of night. She could almost hear his ego expanding. "Nory?"

"Yeah. I need to get my car out of sight."

"My 'vette's in there." The last syllable cracked on a yawn.

"Well move it. Please, Gabe. I'm coming in hot. You do not want my car spotted outside your place."

Again there was silence while he digested that little tidbit. Her tires hit a bump and the shifter's head bounced against her arm.

"Is this an otherworldly kind of thing?" Now fully alert, his voice thrummed with excitement. His footsteps padded down his steps.

Lenore clenched her jaw, drawing on the little scraps of patience she had for the man. Gabe dug all things supernatural. Their short relationship only lasted as long as it did because he was enamored with her being a real-life healer.

"Yes."

He practically squeaked like a girl. She imagined him fist-pumping the air. "How close are you?" Through the phone she heard the rumble of his garage door lifting and the engine of his corvette turn over.

"Two minutes."

She sped down his street, past the white corvette parked out front, her tires squealing on his short driveway, and hit the brakes, as the car rolled into the street-level garage of his townhouse.

The garage door rumbled down behind them. Gabe pulled open the passenger door and leaned in, tousled in nothing but plaid boxers. "Whoa, darlin'. You almost hit the wall."

"Help me with him." Opening her door, Lenore ran around the back of the car.

Gabe tapped the shifter's cheek. "He's completely out."

"Drugs." Lenore squirmed between them to assess just how out of it the guy was.

Gabe straightened to his full height, folding his arms over his chest. "You brought an addict to my place?"

Lenore scowled up at him. "Like I would do that. Geez. Not an addict. Someone drugged him."

Gabe crouched back down beside her and took the guy's arm to start tilting him out. "Why?"

Jonesing for all things supernatural, he was going to love this. The entire time they'd been together she tried to keep him out of the otherworldly scene—or rather, spare him from getting on any of the more lowlife of the creature's radar, all while Gabe pushed to be in it. That couldn't be an issue right now. She needed his help.

"The drugs subdued him. To keep him from properly—Look, they just needed him calm and incoherent long enough to sell."

"Sell?" Gabe's brows rose into the blond streaks at his hairline. "As in human trafficking? Nory, what have you gotten into?"

She winced. "Not exactly human trafficking."

Gabe's head swung toward the huge man crammed in her car, and then back to her, his features impassive, waiting for an explanation. She hated how he did that.

"Shapeshifter, all right. I bought him. I didn't know what else to do."

"You bought a shapeshifter? You can do that? Bought him for what?" His eyes widened with each question uttered. She wasn't sure whether from excitement at seeing a real life shapeshifter or horror at what she'd done.

"I had to. They were going to give him more drugs—and he really can't take any more and survive—and then this weird motorcycle gang showed up, shooting streams of light capable of throwing around the ogres…"

"Wait. What?" Strong hands clamped onto her shoulders and gave a little shake. "Nory, sweetheart, you are not making a lick of sense. Ogres and motorcycle gangs? Okay. Okay. Calm down. We're going to get this guy inside—shapeshifter." A bemused smile lifted his lips. He shook his head, beaming. "Shapeshifter."

Lenore gave him a bland stare.

"Yeah, I know, all right." He lifted the guy's feet out of the footwell. "Let's get him upstairs and then you tell me all about it over a cup of tea." Tugging the shifter's arm, Gabe swiveled him across his shoulder into a fireman's hold, and standing, headed toward the stairs.

Her adrenaline crashing, Lenore followed sluggishly after. "But you hate tea."

Chapter Three

Gabe lowered the shifter onto his bed and stared down at him.

"He's not going to shift." Lenore knelt on the mattress and swept the man's sweat-soaked hair from his clammy face.

"One can hope," Gabe said. "He going to be all right?"

Lenore shrugged with one shoulder while checking the shifter's pulse. It still ran fast, assuming shapeshifter's hearts pumped at a similar rate to a human's. She frowned. "They gave him a high dosage. He just needs to work it out of his system and I'll know more."

"Well, can't you…you know?"

Her teeth pulled across her bottom lip. "Heal him?"

"Well?"

The thought had occurred to her. "Honestly, I don't know. It's not exactly an injury or illness. Can you get me some lukewarm water and washrags?"

"Sure." Gabe's bare feet padded across the tile. She heard cupboards opening and the faucet turn on.

The light from the hallway cast a soft glow over them. The shifter looked vulnerable and young in his sleep again. How did he do that? Go from youthfulness to dripping with masculinity just by opening his eyes? Dark lashes formed feathery half-moons on his perspiring skin.

An urge to help him swelled low in her belly.

Gabe brought in a bowl of water, a couple of towels and several wash cloths. He sat on the other side of the unconscious man, one leg bent on the bed. "So what do we do?"

"Keep him cool. Hydrate him whenever he wakes." She reached over him and took a soaked cloth and began cooling down the guy's arm. "And we can't let him shift. No matter what."

Gabe's gaze snapped up. "Thought the drugs kept that from happening." He dropped another cloth into the water to soak it.

Lenore trailed her cloth down the shifter's nose. He had a nice nose. "They usually do, but earlier, he started to shift anyway. It shouldn't have been possible." She reached across the guy's chest and latched onto Gabe's wrist. "He's strong. Even with the drugs, he would have gone into a transformation."

"And that's bad."

Lenore chuffed. "Not if you want a drugged-out dragon breathing fire in your bed." Or worse, dissipating to nothing. Panic forced her lungs to squeeze. She could barely breathe. She didn't know this guy, but the thought of him fading away to nothing disturbed her on a base level she didn't understand.

"Really?" Gabe's head canted. His eyes gleamed. "Dragon? He could do that?"

Lenore smiled. "I don't know. Probably." The general public didn't realize it, but dragons were real, a few still existed. Most slumbered in their ancient holes deep within the earth.

"Think he'd, after he's back to himself of course, think he'd mind…"

"What? Putting on a show for you?"

"Well, yeah." He dribbled water onto the shifter's flat stomach. "That'd be awesome."

Some things never changed. "You're on your own with that. I'm not asking him."

Gabe smiled indulgently. "You don't think I will?"

"Oh, I know you will. So good luck with that. Hope he doesn't take offense."

Water splashed as he swirled his cloth back into the bowl. "You know no one can resist when I ask nicely."

She certainly hadn't been able to.

Yeah, if anyone knew how to coax his way into getting what he wanted, it was Gabe. Just ask the other two girls he was dating while they were together. The louse. They'd never agreed to be exclusive. Gabe claimed she'd been the longest most serious relationship he'd endured. Endured. Hell of a way to put it. And he'd been charming and reasonable when he said it. He almost made her feel like her way of thinking had been skewed.

He graced her with his patented you-know-you-adore-me grin. "So right now shifting is bad. How will we know if he tries?"

"He'll start to glow. If he does, we have to snap him out of it fast. Quit smiling, this is serious."

"I know, but babe, the entire time we were together, you never did anything like this for me. It's not even my birthday and you brought me a shapeshifter."

"I did not bring him here for you. I needed help."

"And you thought of me first."

She wanted to be mad, but it was true. For all Gabe's faults, she knew she could trust him. With this anyway. "Yes. I thought of you." Her throat tightened. He was an idiot, a flirt and completely untrustworthy as a boyfriend, but he would also give the shirt off his back for anyone in need. "Gabe, thank you for this. Really."

His eyes softened and he leaned over the shapeshifter and kissed her. "Darlin', I'll always be there for you."

"Ugh. I know, which makes you so irritatingly difficult to hate."

He pulled back, eyes dancing. "Then quit trying. You know I'll take you back anytime."

She snorted. "Me and anyone else who catches your attention."

He spread his arms wide. "Love's a beautiful thing. Should be spread around."

"The same is said about manure."

"Ouch."

She leaned closer. "Never going to happen."

"Until the day you realize you can't go on without me." His teeth gleamed in the low light.

"Gabe, you are such an—"

The shifter moaned. Every muscle in his body tightened and started jerking.

"Shifting?" Gabe pressed the man back down.

"Seizure." Lenore's heart rammed up her throat.

"Can you help him?"

Her head snapped up. "I don't know. Maybe." She was going to give it her best shot. Her mouth was bone-dry. "This is going to get bad."

It did get bad.

The poor guy curled in on himself so tight every tendon in his neck and arms stood out white. The bed sheets were wet with sweat and water, his dark hair plastered to his face while his jaw clenched so hard, Lenore worried he'd bite his tongue. His body was bowed so hard, he seemed to be all sharp angles, jutting bone, and bulging veins over tight dry skin.

Gabe stayed with them the entire time, a steady presence while she held the shifter's forehead and whispered soothing nonsense about movies or the upcoming playoffs he'd miss if he didn't hang on. She didn't even know his name. You go through something like this with someone, and you should know their name.

When his eyes suddenly rolled back in his head and his body jack-knifed into a particularly strong seizure, Lenore couldn't let this go on.

Though scared of getting lost to it, she plunged her palm against his clammy chest and forced her essence into him. She wasn't the strongest of healers, but she'd do what she could, if anything.

Dazzling light engulfed her, more vibrant and rich and alive than any essence she'd ever touched. Fluctuating blues and emerald greens.

He was beautiful.

The magic of his shapeshifting abilities was exquisitely pure, untouched by the darkness of the world.

How was that possible?

Were all shapeshifters like this?

No, the thought came unbidden. It's him alone, his soul.

He was honey and spice, protective warmth and intrinsic light chasing shadows. He was playful happiness and devoted worshipful younger brother. Those he loved, he loved deeply with a patience and strength as vast as the world.

She wanted to weep.

Wanted to pour everything that she was into his being and stay right there, tucked within him. She'd never experienced anything like it.

There was no way she'd ever let his soul fade out of this world. No way.

The seizures trembled around her, rough, jerky instable lightning stabs.

Bearing down, Lenore pushed her magic further into his body, gliding her healing across enflamed bone and muscle tissue, like kneading fingers. She had to get this right. Mucking around in someone's body, knitting bone or flesh, or popping blood vessels was a delicate thing. Too much pressure or not enough and a healer could do more harm than good. Fortunately, he wasn't injured, just suffering through withdrawals. Withdrawals that were tearing his muscles apart and searing through his overtaxed nerves. Pain flared through him as intangible streaks of brutal red jabs.

She found the tanglewort flooding through his veins and began gently drawing it out, coaxing it to filter out his pores, while at the same time she slipped her own essence around the nerve cells that were sending out pain signals to his brain. Yeah, she was a supercharged endorphin enhancer. Better than morphine. She felt the immediate response from him as he shivered beneath her inner ministrations and finally unclenched. The shaking abated. His essence flared around her, flashing brighter and pulling her magic within his own, folding her in safe.

Who was supposed to be helping who?

She could easily melt right into him and be content

forever.

Whoa. Dangerous thought. Better get a handle on her own endorphins.

She had to pull back, get out, right the freak now.

She forcefully untangled herself and dragged her magic away, though the desire to remain, just curl up and be, nearly overwhelmed her.

She didn't like it one bit.

Lenore pulled harder...and with a gurgling sputtering plop, came back to herself, half-curled over the guy, lungs heaving for air. It was like stumbling out of a sauna into the rain.

Gabe held her by the shoulders, keeping her from falling all the way onto the shifter.

"You okay?"

She looked up at him through strands of wet hair. The colors of the paint on his walls began seeping back in. He seemed genuinely concerned, as though her well-being was as important to him as the healing process he loved to witness. She'd only used it on him in small short bursts before, like easing headaches or muscle aches.

One side of his lips quirked up. "That was incredible. Did you know the air shimmers around you when you do that?"

"No." She frowned. News to her. "I'm usually a little too occupied to notice. Shimmers?" She'd never seen Charity shimmer. Or her grandma. She looked down at the shapeshifter. It could have been an effect from healing him.

"Yeah. Like looking through the exhaust behind a jet engine." His fingers skimmed her again. "It was sexy."

And he's back.

"It work?" Gabe eyed the man between them. "He went all limp all of a sudden. He going to be okay?"

"Yes." That came out on a swell of determination. He had to be all right. She wouldn't let someone with his force of spirit not be okay.

Gabe leaned back, his gaze far too perceptive.

She looked away, dropping a hand to the shifter's forehead and again that spark of—something—trilled between them. Sticking her finger in a light socket would be less electrical. Ignoring it, she tried to sound professional. "I don't know. I think he'll be fine. I was able to help his muscles relax and in turn, hopefully lower his blood pressure. It's up to him now to ride out the drug's withdrawal."

Gabe nodded. "How 'bout that cup of tea now?"

"Gosh, yes." She wasn't about to move off that bed. Her arms felt like jelly.

Gabe stood and padded across the floor, pausing in the doorway to give her another once over. She must look as wrecked as her bones felt. Warmth flushed inside her belly at the thought of Gabe making tea for her, at the thought that he still kept tea in his cupboards since his beverage of choice had always been cola or beer.

"Mmmmmph." The shifter's hand flopped from his stomach to the mattress. Long lashes fluttered and his features screwed up with pain.

Instantly alert, Lenore scooted closer, resting her palm over his heart, waiting for his muscles to seize and spasm again, though she wasn't sure how much good she could do for him. Her healing strength was all but depleted.

His head rolled against her other palm and he cried out, "Edeen, nay," along with a string of other nearly incoherent phrases.

"Is that Scottish?" Gabe appeared in the doorframe, a steaming mug in one hand, a cola can in the other.

"Shhh, shh, all's well," she cooed to the shifter, pushing sweat-dampened hair from his face, then to Gabe, "He has a deep brogue. Like my grandmother's."

Gabe set the tea and cola on an overturned crate he used for a nightstand. "Real deep."

She scrunched her nose. "His words are slurring with Gaelic and some other language I'm unfamiliar with." As healers, her grandmother insisted both she and Charity learn the basics of several old languages for the simple spells and incantations sometimes required to enhance a difficult healing. Some of the languages weren't meant for mortal ears, like the speech pattern he kept slipping into—*language of the Fae*, her grandmother's voice whispered.

Brows furrowed, Lenore tried to make out his distressed muffled words until her sister's name spilled out on a gasp and all other thoughts were pushed away.

Charity.

Lenore met Gabe's puzzled gaze across the man's thrashing body.

What in the world was going on?

Chapter Four

Near dawn, the shifter finally quieted. His heartbeat maintained a steady rhythm that Lenore assumed was normal. Most importantly, he slept peacefully, without twitches or delirium. She was pretty sure the tanglewort had cleared his system.

She was beat. Sometime after things had gotten quiet, she'd used Gabe's shower, borrowed one of his shirts and gotten an hour's worth of sleep.

She woke beside the shifter and immediately checked his vitals. He looked much better, though exhausted. The pale cast to his skin had lessened significantly, giving way to a healthy tan. The guy must spend a lot of time outdoors. He had scruffy stubble, could definitely use a fresh shave and Lenore wondered when his last one was. If she knew Starch, he would've had that taken care of while he was out to *pretty* him up some. Pretty him up even for her, knowing his youthfulness and beaten state would get to her. Calculating ogre. He'd probably be great at staging furniture showrooms if human and drug trafficking didn't work out for him.

The shifter most likely wouldn't awaken for hours yet, which gave her enough time to settle with Starch and get back here and find out what he had to do with her sister.

Ah, man, Charity. Big Sis should be up by now. It was

her day to open the shop.

Scrambling off the bed, she grabbed her jeans draped over a half-open drawer and dug in the pocket for her phone.

She punched in the number and waited.

Gabe stumbled in, shirtless and droopy-eyed. His mouth cracked wide in a yawn.

Charity wasn't picking up. Geez, come on. She hung up and hit the button to their herbal shop.

"Problem?" Gabe plopped his butt on the end of the bed, making the shifter's foot bounce.

Lenore punched the phone off. "Charity's not answering." She stepped into her jeans. Gabe's sleepy gaze followed their movement up her hips.

She rolled her eyes. "Can you watch him until I get back?"

"Shapeshifter." Gabe's eyes danced. "Hell, yes, I can watch him. Think he'll wake any time soon?"

Lenore hesitated, suddenly uncomfortable leaving the guy. Not that she didn't trust Gabe. She did. The most he'd do is pester the shifter. But leaving the guy when he was vulnerable and there were ogres and yuppies gunning for him…

The ogres she could take deal with. If she got a move on. He was safe here. No one knew where he was. And once she paid Starch off, that would be one less party after the guy. Hopefully the yuppies had gotten bored and sought their entertainment elsewhere. Her gut twisted, imagining what type of entertainment the wealthy young trio had wanted with a drugged-to-the-gills shapeshifter. None of the thoughts were good. That was messed up.

She leaned over the bed to check the guy's pulse and breathing again. "He'll probably sleep a few more hours. I'll be back before then. Don't wake him."

Gabe grinned. "Now why would I do that?"

"I mean it. He could be dangerous. I don't want you hurt."

Gabe's grin widened. His palm splayed over his smooth chest. "You still care. So there's hope for us."

Lenore laughed. "You're such a jerk. Yes, I care. No, we will never get back together. Ever. You're a good guy, Gabe, but you're also a royal pain. I need to borrow your car." And keep hers safely hidden in his garage.

"Keys are in the bowl." He leaned forward, snagging her by the hem of his T-shirt she wore. "Looks good on you."

Rejected and not breaking stride. The guy was incorrigible. He must have an extra flirting chromosome. He simply didn't register the word "no". It was like talking to a wall. A wall with the elevated hormones of a teenager.

"Thanks." Satisfied with the shifter's pulse, she absently ran a hand along his jaw. Her heart took a little tumble as he rolled his face unconsciously into her touch.

"Huh." Gabe snorted.

Lenore snapped her hand away and Gabe laughed. "I saw that."

"What? Get real. I don't even know him."

"Uh-huh."

"I don't."

He stood and drew her up by the shoulders, looking as serious as she'd ever seen him. "For once, sweetheart, just go with what you're feeling without analyzing it." He kissed her forehead. "You might have the best time of your life."

"There's more to living than always looking for a good time," she murmured.

"Life's in the journey," he countered.

"That's all blissful and good until someone gets hurt."

He stared at her for a long moment. "For what it's worth, Nory. I never went out of my way to hurt you."

"No. But you still did."

Chapter Five

Lenore slid into the white corvette, hoping the yuppies hadn't been able to follow or track her. That was assuming Starch hadn't given them her identity, which, with how angry he'd been at the Barbie doll crew shooting up his place, she doubted it. She supposed if the ogre betrayed her, it wouldn't have been hard to locate her by the GPS on her phone. No one had come for them so far, so the novelty for the yuppies had probably worn off for them and they'd called it a night.

Except the uneasiness pinching her lips tight wouldn't let it go at that.

Regardless, all she had to do was get Starch his money and get back to the shifter and find out what his interest in Charity was about. Then he could be on his way.

Funny, she didn't consider that he meant her sister any harm—not after glimpsing the core of his essence.

Heat flushed through her at the memory of her magic entwined with his. Gah, *magic entwined*...crimony.

She nearly missed a turn and jerked the wheel hard to make it. Gabe's work-out bag slid off the passenger seat to the footwell with a plunk.

She had to get it together and stop mooning over how wonderful being inside the shifter's essence felt. Grabbing her phone, she quickly called Starch. She got a busy signal from him too. Was no one going to answer this morning?

She shoved the cell back into her jeans and then pulled the car into her space at the apartment complex.

She'd barely gotten inside, taken her emergency stash from the inside of the toilet paper spinner on the wall and jammed that in her pocket with the rest of the cash, when her doorbell buzzed. She nearly jolted out of her skin.

The ringer buzzed again, followed by frantic knocking.

"Lenore, are you in there?" Charity called. "Answer your door!"

The knob rattled as her sister undoubtedly got fed up waiting and had pulled her spare key out.

Lenore yanked the door open, and Charity spilled inside, her fingers on the key still in the doorknob.

Relief flooded Lenore's vocal chords. "I called you. Several times. Why didn't you pick up?"

"You won't believe what happened." Charity raced down the hall, a disheveled whirlwind of dark hair. "This guy just—" She spun back to face her and threw out her hands. "—just appeared in my kitchen, completely naked, was just all of a sudden there."

"What?" Lenore's heart dropped. Had the yuppies found Charity instead of her? Why would they get naked? "Someone broke in? Are you okay?"

"No. Yes, yes, I'm okay. No, he didn't break in. I'm telling you he just materialized in my apartment. Before my eyes. Out of thin air." Charity's shoulders went up and down in her frantic excitement.

The walls seemed to tilt sideways as Lenore tried to make sense of what she was hearing. "What?" Because really, *what?*

Charity's laugh held a touch of hysteria. She grabbed Lenore's arms to pull her into the library-slash-dining nook. "A sorcerer, Lenore. From the past. One strong enough to open a time rift and seek out a healer."

Lenore sank down into a chair at the little table, processing as Charity chattered about witches and dungeons, broken bones and her healing abilities enhanced times thousands. Old magic from centuries past. Pure unadulterated magic of light. A wounded Highland sorcerer who traveled through time for a respite from the tortures he was even now enduring—well, in his time—at a witch's hand. A witch he could not escape without placing his siblings and clan and the magic they guarded at a higher risk.

And she had a name.

Toren Limont.

Lenore flinched in her seat. She knew that name. Had heard of the last High Sorcerer. But it couldn't be possible.

She spun out of the chair to quickly search the

bookshelves. Where was it? Where was it? Her flea-market shelves were crammed with old texts, even scrolls, anything she could get her hands on. The art of healing fascinated her.

"I can't believe it. One of the fabled sorcerers of Limont came to you. In the flesh."

Her body hummed with the possibility of this being true. Ah, there. She tugged the large tome from among others on the second highest shelf.

"In nothing but his flesh." Charity grabbed the other side of the old book and together they brought it to the table.

"You sure it's in here?"

"Oh yeah, I remember reading about it when I first convinced mom to let me look at the book." It was impossible. The name had to be a coincidence. No way had the High Sorcerer of Limont time-traveled into Charity's apartment. Things like that didn't happen anymore. Not on days when she had a mysterious man of her own to figure out. One looking for Charity.

"You were ten."

Huh? Oh. Lenore shrugged a shoulder. "It was a romantic story, an entire clan, every individual gifted with some form of magic as long as they remained the protectors of man... And then all of them vanished. Poof." It was an incredible story, like a fairy tale. "The village must have fallen to ruin because no one knows where it once was."

She took her gloves from the little carved box on the table. The pages were too old to let the oils in her fingers damage them.

"That's so weird." Charity plunked down beside her. "What does that even mean? Protectors of man?"

"Got me. Something about the innate balance of magic. As long as the Limonts kept the dark side of magic from overtaking the good, the entire land would prosper."

The writing was Gaelic. Their grandmother insisted they learn a bit of many ancient runes and symbols so they could pick out healing spells and incantations. Although they weren't witches, sometimes reciting the words enhanced the little they could do with their natural abilities.

"Magic would remain abundant and the flip side of magic, like the dark fairies, ghouls, and vampires wouldn't get much of a foothold in the world. Here it is." Lenore grabbed her reading glasses and slipped them on. She found what she'd been looking for. Genealogical records.

"Toren Limont," Charity whispered, her head next to Lenore's as they read. "High Sorcerer of Limont, born in Crunfathy. Have you ever heard of Crunfathy?"

"No. Never." Lenore's pulse thundered. What was going on? A shiver of dread swept along the back of her neck. She moved her gloved fingers across Charity's. "You okay?"

"Yeah." Charity's eyes were huge. The tips of her dark hair swished over the velum page and Lenore didn't have the energy to worry about what that could do to the pages. "It's just weird, you know?"

"Do you want to stop?" *Please stop.* Whatever was going on, they weren't a part of it. Not anymore. The sorcerer was back in the past where he belonged. They had more important concerns. On any other day, she'd be all over this, but her priority had to center on finding out what a shifter from Oregon wanted with her sister. And at the same time, keep Charity unaware of her extracurricular activity in procuring needed substances for their seedier clientele.

Tomorrow. She'd help Charity figure this all out tomorrow. They could have a sister's night of it, order Chinese, turn up the tunes, and dig through every book or scroll she had on the ancient Highland clan. Studying, uncovering buried truths, now that was a good time.

If Clan Limont really was the balance that kept dark magic from overtaking the light, they'd done a terrible job of it.

Creatures of dark magic were everywhere.

"No, I want to know what happened." Charity got that stubborn jut to her chin. There'd be no stopping her, which meant simply diverting her for a while.

"All right." She'd get her sister her answers and let her stew on it all day while she rushed to take care of everything else. She twisted her hair into a knot and jammed a pencil in it to keep it on top of her head away from the precious pages. "Your Toren was the last known sorcerer before the clan vanished for good. You see these other names below his?"

Charity squinted.

Lenore traced the names with the tip of the glove.

Toren Limont

Shaw Limont

Edeen Limont

Col Limont

Edeen?

Blinking rapidly, the runes blurred. She shook her head to settle her vision, waiting for the room to quit tilting and stared at the names.

She steadied her breathing. She had things to attend to. "He had two brothers and a sister. It looks like that together the four siblings kept their people safe and the balance of magic in check. They also..." She had to admit, this next part was cool. It was cool when she'd read about it at ten and it was still cool now. "They also each had their own unique brand of magic. The sister was an empath."

"She could tap into other people's emotions," Charity supplied.

"Yes, but back then when magic was part of everyday existence and so much stronger, an empath would have been able to do way more than feel emotions. We're talking the ability to really get into people's heads, dive into memories they don't even know about if she wanted to."

The room suddenly grew warmer, remembering the similar experience she'd had in the wee hours last night. She hadn't experienced the shifter's memories or anything like that, but she'd felt him, everything he was, and…was perspiration coating her forehead? She barely heard what Charity said.

"…touched one of us, she'd see everything we know?"

Yeah, uh, right. "Yes. Can you imagine our healing potential if we lived back then?" She hoped she was on the same topic as Charity, but her sister was so rattled by her own evening's encounter she hadn't yet noticed how tense Lenore was. "Magic was in everything, as simple as plucking it from the air." She smiled. That really would be awesome. She imagined how much more successfully she'd be able to help those who needed her. With that strength of magic she would have been able to draw the tanglewort right out of the shapeshifter instead of her magic barely sufficing as a bandaide while watching—feeling—him suffer.

"So your Toren was the sorcerer, Edeen an empath. The youngest brother Col, was a shapeshifter..." She swallowed past the lump in her paper-dry throat. An unexpected worry needled at her.

Just what she didn't need, another shapeshifter to worry about.

Everything was off, happening all at once. She'd had a harried night. That was all. Hardly any sleep.

"And Shaw: moon sifter."

Her glasses slipped down her nose.

"Which is?" Charity's nose wrinkled.

"I have no idea." But as soon as she had some time, she was going to hit the books and find out. Kay, Charity had her answers. Time to get her out of here and go take care of business. The shifter could have awakened by now. No calls from Gabe yet, so maybe not.

She slipped off her gloves. "So now you know. Your visitor really was a Highland Sorcerer, last of his line before the entire Clan Limont vanished and magic hasn't been as potent on the earth since. It's all pretty amazing when you think about it."

"Yeah." Charity sighed. "Amazing."

It was. It really was. If Lenore wasn't up to her eyeballs in her own problems, she'd be grilling Charity for more specifics. "Hey." She pushed stray strands of her sister's hair behind her ear. "It is amazing. It's not every day things like this happen."

"I know."

"You did what you could for him. And you got to feel incredible power flow through you, more than either of us could generate in these days. That had to feel awesome, right? I know it's hard when you heal someone. You feel like you're responsible for them, but there's nothing more you can do. It's not like you can travel back through time and check on him."

She didn't like the look on her sister's face. "We have time-travel spells. Grandma's done it."

No way. What was Charity thinking? It wouldn't matter anyway. Sorcerers were the only ones who could once open time rifts and there hadn't been any around with enough magic to do that for a couple of centuries anyway. Sure, a talented healer or witch could recite a specific incantation to travel back a few hours, a day maybe, but that didn't have anything to do with messing around with a time rift. Whatever Charity had considered on the spur of the moment wouldn't work anyway. There was nothing to get antsy over.

Lenore eased back in her seat and took her glasses off. "She went back half a day to stop Uncle Frank from getting in that car accident that took his leg. Even if you could pull it off, what would be the point in going back to last night and your Highlander? You've already done what you can for him." She was rambling now, her nerves and emotions fried. "It's not like we have the ability or spells to travel across centuries. Not even the sorcerers of today have the juice to do that anymore."

Charity frowned at the page.

"I'm sorry," Lenore said. "I get it, but it's not possible so there's no use in worrying about him anymore. Whatever happens—happened—to Toren Limont is out of your hands. You got to just let it go."

Charity stood and pulled their grandmother's pink book of spells from the lower shelf. "I know, okay. I'm going to take this home, all right?"

The book had the time-travel incantation their grandmother had once used.

Lenore puckered her lips. There wasn't much Charity could do about a sorcerer who'd gone back to the past. Charity was headstrong to a fault, but she wasn't stupid. She'd come to that conclusion on her own and pouring through grandma's book of spells would keep her busy.

"Sure," Lenore said. "Just don't...you know."

Charity frowned. "Like you said, no one has the juice to travel back that far anyway."

Why didn't that make Lenore feel any better?

Chapter Six

Col floated in a sludge pool of misery and disorientation. He knew he dreamed, his mind and body lethargic, caught in the snare of whatever substance they kept pumping into his arm. Nothing made sense since he'd been flung through the time rift that had opened with the ill-conjured unleashing of magics between the witch Aldreth and his brother Shaw while they'd battled upon Crunfathy Hill.

That rift had been unnatural, felt wrong, pulling him apart at his most basic essence before spitting him out in this cold distant time.

He'd nearly lost himself to the ether, had barely gathered his particles and solidified, a naked, weak husk, shivering in the dark alley of what he'd surmised at first to be a large keep, but learned in this age of man 'twas a gutted warehouse. Everything was strange and dark, a noisy rain-soaked land brimming with people who'd lost the joy of simply being, and monsters who cavorted with the unsuspecting mortals like wolves moving downwind among sheep.

The magic of the earth had grown dark. The air quivered with the tainted imbalance, thrumming deep and heavy against Col's essence.

They had failed.

His family had failed.

Whatever had transpired in his time, he knew his family—the guardians of the Fae's magic—had failed to keep the balance between light and dark magics.

He had to get back home. Mayhap right this.

Which meant finding a sorcerer to create a time rift for him.

Finding garments to clothe himself had been far easier. When he stumbled out of the alley, the first person he came upon lifted a maiden's thin dining dagger to his throat. What could the man possibly have wanted from him in his current state of undress? 'Twas apparent he had nothing of value. More to the point, he had nothing. *By the rood*, these people of the future were suspicious.

Col divested him of his blouse and strange trews instead.

'Twas when he rounded the corner into lighted night, and carriages miraculously pulled without livestock, whirring past, his stomach rose like gore to his throat.

He had traveled far, far beyond his time.

Weeks passed in this new world. He learned to survive in this new age by wit and brawn, scrabbling among the darkest dregs of creatures that had ever been spat from the wombs of magic kind. The odd job for scraps of food and a place to sleep off the cold streets for a night, a brawl for wagerers' entertainment. He moved from city to city, always asking, always searching for an elusive sorcerer, unwilling to believe when all laughed, saying sorcerers no longer had magic.

He couldn't believe that.

He had to get back. Charity had managed it.

Charity. Just like that a new plan was conceived. He wasn't certain of an exact time. He could be decades or centuries off, but he had a name and he had a place, connecting with the lass's unfathomable tale of his brother opening a rift and traveling to the Twenty-first Century to seek a healer for a short respite from the witch Aldreth's tortures.

Toren was coming here. A sorcerer powerful enough to get him home. If, in fact, his brother hadn't already made the journey.

He had to find Charity Greves of Seattle.

That was the plan and how it had all run afoul, Col was yet to make sense of it. 'Twas all a murky blur. He'd gone to a run-down tavern. Seems in any era, pubs and taverns were the place to seek information. He'd barely asked the barkeep of anyone who might know of a healer, specifically one Charity Greves when ghouls set upon him. He'd fought, of course, transformed into one of the large cats of the Highland cliffs and was making a good accounting among the dozen or so wiry beasts, until the troll set his ale down and unfortunately took up the defense of the ghouls. Who would have thought they'd be mercenaries for the same coin? Certainly not him, though by then 'twas too late to sort any sense from it.

Everything had gone to shite after that, fuzzy and muddled. A sharp pain stabbed him and with it a fiery burn that dragged into his veins. They'd given him something. Some potion. He felt it crawl sluggishly through his blood, making his reactions clumsy. It had taken the ghouls moments to overcome him.

Then there'd been darkness and waking times where he'd bounced in the back of an untethered wagon, glimpsing spots of overcast sky through a slanted pane of glass as the carriage carried him away from his search. There'd been harsh voices and harsher treatment, more of the burning potion that turned his thoughts to porridge and a soft voice offering help with a singular burst of energy that pierced his essence with the first moment of clarity he'd had in days.

Then...what?

If the memories before the woman were a haze, everything afterwards reeked of nightmares. Exquisite pain, heat and blistering chills, his body wrenched so tight he couldn't breathe. He could hardly distinguish dream from reality anymore.

Mayhap 'twas all nightmare.

He fought to consciousness, clawing through the shadowy haze that did not want to recede.

He had to get to Charity before Toren came. 'Twas his only hope of returning home and leaving this thrice-cursed century behind.

He drifted upward, expecting to struggle through the lethargy shrouding him.

Movement fluttered near. The padding of feet across a hard floor. He flexed a finger, testing, relieved when his hand obeyed.

Whatever he was laying on shifted beneath another's weight.

Col strained to open his eyes. What new circumstance would he find himself in now? Whatever 'twas, he'd rather not greet it defenseless on his back.

His lashes fluttered, revealing patches of subdued light. A wet cloth slapped upon his chest and started trailing water down his stomach.

"That's it," a male voice muttered. "You can wake up any time. I'm bored. Or does the slumbering prince require a kiss?"

Everything inside Col went on alert. What depth of blackness had he been cast into now?

The dripping cloth circled back up and Col concentrated everything he had to open his eyes. His blurry gaze opened to curious brown eyes staring down on him.

"Hey there." The man grinned beneath wild locks of hair hanging around a lean face. "You back with?"

Col angled upward against protesting muscles and rolled off the other side of the bed, coming up into a defensive stance. A dozen hammers banged inside his skull.

The man flung his palms up, showing he bore no arms, just the wet cloth that fell from lax fingers to plop on the mattress. "Whoa, dude. You look kind of green. You probably shouldn't move so fast."

That was a given. Col narrowed his gaze. Searching the man's scant attire of some sort of thin short breeches for anyplace to conceal blades, he didn't see any. He wondered what clan the tartan design designated. "Who are ye? What do ye want?" And where was the honey-voiced lass who slashed through his bonds and spirited him away within the cramped belly of her wee carriage? *Car*, they called them cars.

He pressed the heel of his hand against his pounding head, trying to make the man's suddenly blurry image solidify. Surely the lass hadn't been a conjuring of his potion-addled mind. He'd felt her. Bone-deep somehow. Experienced the vibrancy of her magic, her desire to help him. She was very real. He'd wager on it.

The man shifted back off the bed, wisely keeping his hands in sight. "Easy. I'm Gabe. This is my house. We've been taking care of you. You've had a rough night. Withdrawals. Spasms. So just take it easy, fella. No one here's out to hurt you."

Thus far, everyone in this century seemed *out to* harm him in one form or another. Snatches of overheard conversations slashed into his thoughts, ugly words of vile intentions. His gaze flicked to the bed.

Gabe crossed his arms. A light brow arched. "Trust me. Don't trust me. It's been a long night and I need coffee." He turned and stalked out the door, rounding back a second later. "Once you get over yourself, you're welcome to some." And flounced away on a chuff.

Col blinked. He'd apparently wounded his captor's feelings.

Yet...he studied the room, the rumpled bedclothes and a bowl of water and cloths on the bed. His body ached like he'd worked the fields from sunrise to sundown, yet the lethargy he'd lived with from the potions they'd shot directly into his flesh from some alchemist's wicked instrument was gone. He was tired, aye, his head ready to splinter, yet he felt more himself than he had in a while.

Mayhap he had, indeed, been freed and this man had helped him at his most vulnerable.

Cautiously, Col went to the doorway. The man, Gabe, sat at a small round table, slunk in his chair, long legs stretched out and hands clasped comfortably on his stomach, facing the bedroom doorway.

A strong aroma lifted with the steam from two mugs set before him.

The man motioned for him to sit in the second chair, all traces of hurt forgotten. "Cappuccino?"

Col lowered into the chair, still wary and tense and

eyed the frothy brew dubiously. Another potion? His stomach rumbled.

Gabe lifted his own cup and took a sip, watching Col over the brim. "Hmmm. I make a fine cup. Not a coffee man? I have juice or pop." He lowered his cup, pursing his lips. "Your stomach queasy after all that puking? I should have asked Nory what's safe for you to eat before she left. How about toast? That should be bland enough." Gabe got up and turned to the long worktable that housed a small watering trough.

She? He hadn't imagined her then. She'd rescued him, unbound his wrists and spirited him away within her wee *car*. He liked *cars*. Col flattened his palms on the table and leaned forward. "Where is the fair lass who gave me aid?"

Gabe half-turned, his features momentarily frozen until a grin melted the coolness. "Fair lass?" He pulled an already sliced wedge of bread from a transparent satchel and plopped it in a strange metal square. "Seriously. Do all shapeshifters talk like that?"

Col frowned. "What's wrong with my speech?"

"For starters...?"

Col leaned forward, curious. He hadn't done a fair job of maneuvering unconsciously through this century. Mayhap in large part due to the strangeness of his dialect. He'd have to do better, mimic what he heard.

The bread popped up from the metal device and Col

lunged out of the chair, sweeping a small glass plate up and breaking it against the table to defend himself. 'Twould saw through skin as well as any blade given enough pressure behind it.

Gabe flinched back, hands up again in a placating gesture, his jaw unhinged, dropping like a stone. They stared at each other until Gabe slowly shook his head. "They really did a number on you, didn't they?" He backed up against the counter, giving Col farther space. "Look. I swear whatever happened to you, whatever you've been through, isn't going to happen here. You're safe, I promise. Take a seat. You look like you're about to keel over."

His weakness was too obvious. Col lowered into the chair again before his legs gave out. Gabe turned back to the counter and slathered butter across the warmed bread, took out a plate and brought it over.

When Col just looked at it, Gabe rolled his eyes and broke off a piece and popped it in his own mouth.

Col's mouth watered. His stomach groaned at the smell of bread. He needed to regain his strength. If the man had wished him harm, he'd had ample opportunity while he'd been unconscious. He set the broken plate down and took a tentative bite of the bread. 'Twas warm and crunchy. He finished it off in three bites and turned his attention to the steaming mug. One eye closed of its own accord at the strong, yet sweet flavor.

Gabe barely masked his grin behind his own cup. "It's

good, right?"

Col nodded curtly, allowing the warmth of the brew to soothe the tension within his chest.

"So, shapeshifter, huh?" Gabe leaned closer over the table. "What's it like?"

Col scrunched his nose, not understanding the inquiry.

"Shifting. Does it hurt? Is it difficult? When you're in the shape of, say a cow, do you retain human thoughts? Or are you like 'hey look at me. I'm chewing cud?'"

A cow. Col hid his smile behind the mug. A cow. He'd never once shifted into something as mundane as livestock. Gabe kept firing questions at him. Apparently, he'd restrained himself until they'd broken bread together and now his dam had burst and flooded the village.

"...the biggest creature you've shifted into and for how long? Have you ever—you know—boinked in animal form?"

Col choked on the liquid.

A dozen soft paper squares were shoved into his hand, which Col assumed were meant to wipe his mouth with. He stared at Gabe, who shrugged as unconcerned as the cat eyeing the laird's falcon.

"Too much too soon?"

Too much ever.

Boinked. He stored the new word away, doubting he'd have need of it in conversation, but, again he smiled, thinking of how using the amusing new word would annoy Shaw to distraction.

Col pushed Gabe's odd questions aside. "The woman who helped me. Where is she?"

A flash of fairy bright hair and wide violet eyes flicked to his mind. In his hazy state, he'd thought her one of the Fae come to claim him. Or come to punish him for allowing the scale of magic to tip so profoundly.

"Nory? She left a while ago. Did what she could as far as healing and skedaddled."

Ske-what? A healer then. Col nodded on a flood of relief that a Healer Sorceress had found him. And felt profoundly saddened that she hadn't remained long enough to accept his gratitude.

Nay, he was saddened that she simply hadn't remained. Gratitude or no. His lips quirked downward at the unbidden thought. *Nory.*

He pushed it away to brood on later. Or never. There were graver things that needed his attention. His captivity had taken days from him. Days in which Toren may have already traveled the rift, come, and then gone.

He pushed up from the chair a little too fast. Pain flared inside his head and the colors in the room faded. He braced his hands on the table and let it pass. *By the rood*, he felt wretched.

His head felt like it was wrapped in fabric, heavy and disorienting. He had no idea of what to do next or where to look for a sorcerer or Charity. For that matter he had no inkling of where he was.

Gabe was looking at him in concern a little too closely. "I—Which village is this?"

Gabe's lips twisted. "I wouldn't exactly call Seattle a village."

Everything in Col tensed, then just as swiftly loosened. "Seattle? This is Seattle?" That was the best piece of fortune he'd had since being thrust into this nightmare future.

His mind was swimming with possibilities. Gabe was acquainted with at least one Sorceress Healer, mayhap he also knew…"Charity Greves. Do ye know the lass?" His knuckles ground against the table as he leaned forward.

"Yeah, sure." Gabe set his mug down. "I know Charity."

Chapter Seven

Col leaned harder on the table, weak with sudden relief. "Ye must take me to her at once. Is she still here?" This was the first person who claimed to know aught of the lass. He could reach Charity. He could go home.

Gabe lunged out of his seat, eyes narrowed as he stared at him across the small table. "What exactly does that mean—still here?"

"It means I need to get to her forthwith. Please."

"No. No way. Lenore will have my sac in a—"

The window beside them shattered, spraying them and the table in glass shards. A dark leathery creature crashed through the frame, dragging Gabe to the floor. Col grabbed the broken plate and stabbed it into the beast's shoulder since its shoulder was right there, and pulled the monster off, thrusting it away as more creatures surged through every window. Breaking glass and heavy thumps came from the other rooms.

Wrinkled bloated faces, more suited for drowned corpses, followed them. Puckered skin flowed over the hollow space of the eye sockets like translucent veined scar tissue poorly healed. Whether they were blind or nay, it didn't slow them. They could just as easily detect them by scent through the upturned nostrils. The creature Col had knocked off Gabe scrambled up onto the counter, screeching. Two more edged toward them, long curved black glistening toenails scratching the floor.

Grabbing Gabe's arm, Col pulled him up off the floor. The monsters snarled in unison, transparent bloodless lips rippled back over braces of sharply pointed pewter gray teeth. It did not require much imagination to know what those teeth were for. "I need a sword."

"Sorry, all out." To his credit, Gabe's voice remained steady. "Butcher knives?" He canted his head toward short hilts of varying sizes protruding from a block of wood on the work counter near the water trough. Unfortunately, the creature was nearly on top of it.

More beasts showed up from the other rooms, hedging Col and Gabe into a tight space. Col watched the shifting of their long claw-tipped hands, the way their heads tracked toward the one near the knives. The leader. Awaiting its signal.

In all his life, he'd never seen creatures such as these. And he had known many of the otherworldly. They appeared smaller, sleeker, than they actually were, with shoulders hunched inward and rounding their spinal columns. Should they stand up straight, Col guessed they'd tower over him and Gabe. Even their hairless heads covered in moist bloated skin, hung below the curved line of their shoulders like gruesome cowls.

Vile, disgusting, slavering beasts didn't describe them by half. Most noticeable was the wave of stink emanating off them. It stained the air like oily smears. If evil ever were to acquire a smell, this was it. Copper tang of old blood and decaying graveyards.

Col edged toward the leader, watching for any telltale sign of the order to attack and nudged his shoulder slightly in front of Gabe. He longed for the familiar presence of his brothers beside him, in fact, usually finding himself the one nudged back as they were always so recklessly ready to shield him, the youngest among them.

The creature launched. All the beasts flew at them. Col dodged, shoving Gabe down. Claws dragged across the top of his hair. He dove toward the wood block, and whirled back around, blades in both hands and slashed a silver edge across the creature's muscled clavicle as it pounced back at him.

Sticky pale gray blood spurted across his face. The stink alone would do him in. Another creature leapt onto his back. Going to a knee, Col curled forward and let the beast's own weight carry it over his shoulder where it tumbled into Gabe who'd found his own short knife and stabbed upward, coating his arms in noxious ropey excrement that slurped out into a steaming pile on the floor. Gabe's eyes rounded. At least the hell-spawns had the decency to sport skin that parted easily enough. Though their wounds didn't seem to slow them. Parchment skin, leather hard insides. 'Twas not a favorable composition for putting them down. Their numbers alone would eventually overwhelm them.

They slashed and gouged, yet the beasts kept coming. 'Twas the close quarters that gave he and Gabe any leeway, keeping the horde from swarming over them completely. They fought side by side, yet in the fray, Col noticed the monsters' intent was fastened solely on getting at him. They certainly did not oppose swiping at Gabe; yet he appeared to be more of an obstacle to getting at him.

Gabe cried out, bone crunching, his leg buckling beneath him. A beast had dived in, breaking his naked thigh between his long hands like a twig, sending Gabe down. A vulnerable target, yet instead of going for the kill, the monster scurried over Gabe to dive at him.

He spun quickly away, hearing the pleasing thud of the beast slamming into the work counter.

"Get under the table!" Col roared, pulling away and dragging several hellions with him.

Every head swiveled to him, scrabbling along the counters and up the walls to get at him, squealing and hissing as he kicked and stabbed, dislodging two, three, while more clamored over him. He'd been right. They had no interest in Gabe.

Claws bit deep, cutting his skin. 'Twas time to take flight. Literally.

He went down in a jumble of foul-smelling flesh, slick with greasy blood, his and theirs.

Gathering his essence into his core, he let it loose,

allowing the whole of his magic to pour through him. Focused, he brought the image of the bear he'd hunted last fall to mind, became pure bright humming energy that instantly parted into an agony of shifting muscle and bone.

He came up growling, teeth, fur, lethal claws, and furious.

Monsters somersaulted through the air.

Gabe popped his head out from beneath the table, mouth forming something akin to, "Blessed shite."

Only momentarily put off, hissing, teeth gnashing, the creatures regrouped, and surged over Col. Giving into the primitive nature of the bear, he ripped into them, knives forgotten, fighting with his new weapons of nature, jaws and claws. Noxious gore filled his mouth, dripped down his throat.

He had to draw the beasts out of here, but he didn't know the way out for this behemoth form.

He gutted another creature, throwing it into the wall, where it smacked and slid down in a trail of milky gray entrails, scattering beasts beneath it. Col abruptly found himself without opponents.

Only a handful remained, edging along the walls and counter, hissing and spitting at him.

Gabe pushed up, favoring his leg, little knife out front, his attention focused on him.

The remaining monsters were a little more wary, snapping and goading each other to make a move at the towering bear. Not wasting the momentary lapse, Col shifted again, slicing into brilliant energy and coming out the other side in full flight, flapping wings as a hawk and streaked out the broken window.

He wasn't above a little goading himself. Shrieking, he back-flapped, hovering in the air, taunting the beasts to follow him.

They did not disappoint, catapulting after him, clambering out the windows, down the walls, and launching through the air to clasp upon tall poles topped with the strange glowing lanterns.

Col darted low, keeping himself in easy sight to lead them on a merry chase.

Chapter Eight

Something wasn't right. Lenore was halfway to Starch's rendezvous, when she turned the corvette back toward Gabe's. Her stomach clenched on nauseous roiling foreboding, the kind that grips you so hard you'll choke before it can be ignored.

She pulled onto the curb in front of his townhouse and spilled out of the door. Everything looked fine. Scratch that. The blue blinds billowed out of the living room window, clanking against the iron sill. Every window in the townhouse was shattered.

Gabe. Oh no. She'd brought this to him. She ran up the steps and tried the door. Locked. "Gabe!" She pounded on the lacquered wood and poured on the bell. Not waiting, she ran down the steps, jerked open his car and yanked the garage remote from the visor, running and pressing the button at the same time. She ducked under the rumbling garage door while it was still lifting and ran up the stairs.

"Gabe!" She flung the door open so hard it smacked the wall. "Gabe!"

"In here."

Relief smacked her upside the head, making her suddenly woozy. She ran into the kitchen and stopped short.

A powerful stink assaulted her.

Gabe was on the floor, trying to right an overturned chair and push himself up. Trails of thick mucousy gray goo coated everything, including Gabe. His hair was plastered to his head with it and it ran down his face. He grinned up at her like a five-year-old caught licking icing off the cake. The angle of his leg was wrong, clearly broken.

"What happened?" She ducked inside his bedroom, heart plunging at the rumpled empty bed and glass from the broken window covering it. "He's gone?"

"Flew out the window as a little bird." Gabe fluttered his fingers in the air and snorted. "He became a bird."

"A bird?"

Lenore pulled a handful of dish cloths from the drawer and knelt in front of Gabe. Sticky smelly whatever soaked into the knees of her denim. She gave the cloths to Gabe and turned her attention to his leg.

He flinched. "Ow."

"It's broken."

"I'll file that in my *no shit* folder."

She glanced up at him. He was gray-faced, literally from all the crap on him, but stoic and she felt guilty as crap for dragging him into this. "Gabe, what happened? What is this stuff?" The pile of ropey gray matter beside them looked uncannily like sausage. She doubted she'd ever be able to eat a good bratwurst again.

Leaning forward, he grabbed her shoulders. "I'm not

sure even you would believe it. Monsters, Nor, hand-to-God monsters crashed through the windows. It was incredible."

"Monsters?" Gabe hadn't had any previous contact with the supernatural world that he knew about at any rate. Monsters could describe a lot of things. "What were they? Did you get a good look?"

He gave her a you've-got-to-be-kidding glare. "I got a good look, believe me. They were...I don't know...like Morlocks."

"Morlocks?"

"Blind. Leathery. Toothy. Morlocks. Come on, you know what I'm talking about. The misshapen cannibals from *The Time Machine*. Ring any bells?"

Yeah, she knew what Morlocks from the movie were, but no, she had no idea what real mythical creatures Gabe could have described as a Morlock. Ghouls maybe, but blind? How would he know they were blind? What, they came in, feeling their way around? Shock, Gabe was in shock.

"And the shifter...I thought they had him, but he comes up all teeth and claws." Gabe grinned. He busted his leg and was sitting covered in monster innards and the idiot was grinning like a loon. "The guy turned into a bear. A freaking twelve-foot Kodiak! It was amazing. He was beautiful. He shredded into the Morlocks like paper mache."

The shapeshifter shifting into a bear, she got, but Morlock-type monsters? That didn't make any sense. Unless Starch had sent creepers or something after them. Which meant the ogre knew about Gabe when all this time she thought she'd kept him safely out of it. That was a disturbing thought.

Except ghouls or anything she knew about didn't bleed gray.

"Okay, okay." She had to set Gabe's leg. "Where did the shifter go?"

"He turned into a bird." Gabe's eyes darted wildly about the gore-slickened kitchen. "He went anywhere he wanted, taking every last monster with him." Awe floated across his tone. "I didn't think half the Morlocks were still moving. Half of them I thought were disemboweled, but they all got up and went after him. Some limping after him. I doubt they'll get very far, but who knows. They're tough smelly bastards."

Lenore's brows rose. He was really taken with the shifter. Using the distraction while he was relaxed, she quickly pulled his leg into place.

Yelping, his hands knuckled the floor. "A little warning. I swear, you have no bedside manner, anyone tell you that? What happened to your healer's touch, huh?"

"Sorry, I don't have time." She softened. "Want me to jumpstart the bones knitting?"

He frowned, thinking about it. "Is it going to hurt as

much as what you just did?"

She crinkled her eyes in a wince.

"Think I'll go with nature for now, thank you so much." Which was completely unlike him. In the past, he got all jazzed anytime she'd eased a headache for him or anything minor. Her gaze narrowed. He didn't want her expending energy on him right now. He really was concerned about the shapeshifter.

"Okay," she agreed. "Hang on." Spinning, she ran into the bathroom and grabbed the first aid kit from beneath the sink and dragged out an ace bandage roll to stabilize his leg. "I need to know why the shifter is looking for Charity. And why everyone and everything is after him? Did he say anything?"

Gabe's lips pulled down into the equivalent of a facial shrug.

"What?"

"He asked if I knew Charity. Insistently. Said it was life or death."

"Life or death?" Lenore's steam deflated. Whose life and whose death? "This…this is all just a mess. I have no idea what is going on."

"You'll figure it out."

She smiled. "Thanks, Gabe. I hope so, which is why I've got to go. I'm sorry."

"Wait." Gabe pressed his hands on the chair to shift up. "I'm coming."

She pressed him back down. "No. You'll slow me."

"I'll sit in the car."

"This isn't your fight. I shouldn't have involved you in the first place."

"Are you kidding? Best night of my life." He closed one eye, thinking it over. "Well, close second. There was that time in New Hampshire..."

"I don't want to hear it." Only Gabe could find *that* good of a time in New Hampshire. Lenore peered down at Gabe and realized he wasn't joking. His features shone. Clearly she'd underestimated just how much he was enamored by everything otherworldly.

"He shapeshifted in front of me, Nory. I'll never forget that."

Lenore clicked her mouth closed and drew back, thinking. "I can't. Sorry." She had to straighten this out with Starch, whether it was him who sent *monsters* after the shapeshifter or not. She softened her tone. "Trust me, Gabe, you do not want to be part of this world. It's not as cool as you think it is."

"What I saw was pretty damn cool."

"And it almost got you killed."

"Believe it or not, I was holding my own."

She glanced pointedly at his bandaged leg.

"Twenty against two, Nory, and this is all I took."

"Which makes you the walking wounded and trust me on this, where I'm going, all sorts of creatures will hone in on that weakness and will be on you like the last tequila at closing time. Your presence will put me in more danger. Stay here, Gabe. Please."

His mouth thinned into a hard tight line. "Fine. Go. You're going to do what you want anyway." He swiped one of the cloths down his gore-covered face.

Saying anything to soothe him now would be pointless. She grabbed the portable phone where it'd fallen in the corner behind the table by the toaster, checked it for a dial tone, and then handed it to him. "You have someone you can call?" She glanced around at the mess. "For your leg? Who can get you to a clinic."

"I'm not friendless." No. That's one thing she could never accuse him of.

He snagged her wrist. "One hour. Call me in one hour so I know you're all right. You owe me that."

She glanced around the dripping gray-coated countertops and nodded. She owed him much more than that.

Chapter Nine

Col doubled back. He lost the creatures following him in a tangle of alleys and tall buildings, then flew back to the man's—Gabe's—home. He perched in the shadow of a flowering tree. A small flock of sparrows fluttered away, squawking at the intrusion of the large hawk in their midst.

The feral instincts within him honed in on the little birds with intensity.

Tamping the predator down, Col focused on the house, looking for signs that any of the monsters were still around to trouble Gabe. He didn't want that. Not when Gabe was the only person in this ill-forsaken time that had tried to help him.

Not entirely true.

There was the woman, though she was a blurry memory at best of large eyes and wide lips.

There was also the fact that Gabe knew Charity and could direct him to her.

The place was as he left it. Glass strewn beneath the broken windows, but no movement, except for a few of the horseless *cars* that traveled along the quiet hardened roadway. None of the occupants appeared to notice or care that one of their villagers had lost his precious glass panes.

Col curled his talons around the branch, turning his

head to survey the area. It seemed all of the beasts had indeed chased after him. He was about to fly into the window and transform back into himself when the main door opened and the woman who brought him to Gabe in the first place stepped out.

Seeing her, knowing she was real, felt like a punch to his gut. His essence flared within him, the compulsion to change back into a man and reveal himself as he was to her cursedly near overwhelmed his senses.

He shimmered already starting the shift, in total response to her.

He clamped down hard—remaining the hawk. What came over him? To shift while still in a tree? He had more restraint than that.

Her face tilted upward, searching the branches he hid within. Col's tiny avian heart fluttered rapidly in his ribcage. She was beautiful.

More so than he'd given his delirious mind credit for conjuring. She was fine-boned and delicate, as ethereal as the Fae. White-blond hair floated around her like a wispy cloud. He felt pulled toward her, a connection strung taut between them, a frizzle of magical current upon the air.

His wings spread, though he didn't realize he'd moved even a fraction, ready to dive out of the tree to go to her.

Her gaze snapped upward again. A slight frown of puzzlement tilting her slender brow. She looked quickly around some more before climbing into the white carriage that growled to life and carried her away.

Col had a rare moment of hesitation. Follow the woman or stay and get answers from Gabe? He went with his instincts, or rather the urge to keep her in sight if he was honest with himself. Besides, he knew where to find Gabe.

He soared after the low *car*, easily keeping its bright color in the hawk's overly keen sight. She drove into a darker area of town, the streets running with filth, the inhabitants obviously unconcerned with keeping refuse from piling close to their doorways.

Col landed upon the overhang of a window sill as the car rolled to a stop and the woman stepped out.

Looking around warily, she ducked into the shadowed recesses between two close buildings. Col flew over the top to follow her, bristling at the men lounging along the alley walls who whistled and called out to her, waggling fingers in gestures Col had little trouble interpreting. He banked lower, ready to give the ruffians a lesson in the proper treatment of women.

The little Fae's eyes flared with annoyance and she flashed a hand gesture of her own. Col hovered, flapping gusts of air beneath him, mesmerized by the turn of emotions playing across her face.

One of the men pushed off from the wall, stalking toward her. The woman's gaze speared him, large violet eyes widened fractionally and again that searing connection winged across the space separating them as though they were the only two people in the world.

Col dropped low to intervene when a meaty ogre burst through the open door at the end of the alley, shouting and the bludgers scattered.

Col flew into the shadows, alighting on the metal grating of an iron stairway that climbed the side of the building.

"Where's my shifter?" the ogre bellowed.

Col's heart gave a jolt in recognition. 'Twas the gruff voice of one of his captors while he'd been incapacitated beneath the haze of the vile potion.

"Not your shifter. And not your concern." The woman craned her neck back, a waif antagonizing a mountain of unforgiving muscle. He felt a smile try to form if he had a mouth instead of a beak. She pulled out a wad of the thin paper that served as currency. "Bought and paid for. He belongs to me now so you don't need to worry about his whereabouts."

She slapped the paper into the ogre's wide palm.

Col's head went reeling. She purchased him? Like a bauble at market? Had his entire abduction been caused by this one slip of a girl? Why was everyone in this century out to see him harmed?

She poked the ogre's chest. "I trust my money's good enough to keep your gums from flapping. Buyer confidentiality and all that."

The ogre placed a beefy paw over his heart. "Pix, you wound me." His eyes narrowed. "You don't have to worry about them. Those little bikers tried to steal from me. ME! They show their faces around here again..." He didn't finish the statement, didn't need to with how his eyes glittered.

The lass's features relaxed, stirring all sorts of unwanted feelings inside of Col. "Thanks, Starch. So we're good?"

The bulbous head nodded. "I take care of my loyal customers, Pix. Don't doubt me on that." His lips lengthened in a sardonic grin and the woman nodded, turning to go.

She took a different route than the way she came, turning around corners and twisting into thin alleyways barely wide enough for one person.

Flying above, Col kept her in sight until she ducked beneath a low awning and didn't emerge from the other end. He swooped lower, but couldn't find her. She must have entered the building.

He dropped out of the sky the last few feet as a man and stalked beneath the green canvas overhang she'd ducked beneath. There was a door, chained and locked from the outside. Unless she'd used some form of magic, she couldn't have gone in there and then re-chained the doorway from within.

His gaze roamed across every crack and crate leaning against the dirty walls. He couldn't search for long, not in the state of undress shifting left him in. Anyone could come upon him.

Turning, he scrubbed a hand down his face. "What kind of magic is this?"

"The hide in a corner kind." She came out of the shadows where she had tucked her slight form beneath the crate and the door, covering her bright tresses beneath a cowl attached to her blouse. So simple. He felt like a fool.

He was most assuredly grinning like a fool as well, but he couldn't help it, being this near to her.

She held a cylindrical item in her hand with a form of a rather large insect painted on it, thumb on a small tab on top. He had no idea what it could do, but had witnessed enough small weapons of this time wreak surprising damage on creatures much larger than himself. His eyes flicked from the weapon to her face. 'Twas a strike right to his belly, looking at her up close and without the haziness of potions. That strange sensation nearly took him off his feet. Magic streamed between them as though her very essence pierced into his soul and took hold, shaking him to his core and baring everything he was for her to see out in the broad light of day.

Powerful Sorceress. He was weak before her. 'Twas unsettling and wonderful all at once.

He lifted his chin, feigning amusement against her weapons and magic. "What d'ye intend with that?" He kept his voice indifferent.

A small shoulder lifted in a shrug and she pointed the cylinder downward. "You are kind of exposed."

Col felt himself shrivel.

Her eyes tipped back to his face. "What do you want with Charity?" Anger strained the delicate features. Col cocked his head, studying the desperate tension of her limbs. She was scared. Not for herself. Protective. Of Charity.

As was he.

He lifted his palms outward. "I mean her no harm. Ye've my oath on that." His heart pounded just thinking about this one narrow opportunity he had and what would be if he missed it. "She hasn't gone yet, has she?"

"Gone yet?" The color leeched from the lass's skin. "What does that mean?"

His intentions weren't to upset her. He wasn't sure how much to reveal or if he could trust her. She'd purchased him from the ogre, for rood's pity. He should not lose sight of that.

Col looked her up and down, uncertain what to do next. He didn't want to frighten her off, not if she could take him to Charity. Although she obviously didn't frighten easily. Though slight, she'd faced the ogre thrice her size unflinchingly, not to mention an unclothed stranger in a darkened alley.

Fearless, his little Fae was.

She glared at him in silence and then suddenly her eyes widened a fraction and her lips parted.

"Col?"

He flinched at the use of his name. He hadn't heard it for more than a fortnight since he'd been thrown into the rift. No one of this century knew him. Or so he thought.

She must have caught his reaction because her eyes widened larger and she flung a hand over her mouth.

Col's mouth went dry. "You know me?"

"Oh crap," she wailed. "Oh crap, crap, crap. You are him! Col Limont!" A sharp tremor shook her slim frame. "What's going on? How did you get here? What's going to happen to my sister?"

Sister?

He took in her features again, the pert nose and the way she firmed those stubborn lips. He should have realized. Charity's sister. Which…was the most promising event to favor him thus far. As long as he gained the lass's cooperation, he could get to Charity. Get home.

"Ye're Charity's sister then?" He smiled. "Praise the gods. I need to find Charity before…" How much to reveal? "I need to get to her."

"Before what? You need to get to my sister before what? Before your sorcerer brother comes through time? Because he's already done that."

Everything went numb. A sword could have stabbed through him and he wouldn't have felt it. Every thought stilled, save one. "Toren? Toren's already come? And Charity? She's still here?"

"Still here?" the lass shrieked. Her face flushed pink. She aimed her cylinder at him in a shaky hand. "Quit saying that. What do you know? You spill now."

"I—" Col plowed his hand through his hair, reeling. Toren had already come and gone. He'd missed him. He'd missed his chance for Toren to send him home.

He stumbled back, swiveled around, looking for answers on the dirty street that weren't there. A hole as vast as the ocean tore inside his chest. A loud roar thundered in his ears.

He was stuck here. In this hideous time. He'd failed. They'd all failed to maintain the balance of magic. Darkness had overcome the light and there wasn't a cursed thing he could do to set it right.

"Hey, hey." The lass held his arm and was apparently taking the brunt of his weight on her. He hadn't noticed he'd been slowly sinking toward the ground.

The sudden slap on his cheek was more irritating than hurtful. He blinked up.

Frightened violet eyes bore into his. "I don't know what is going on with you and your brother. But you both need to leave my sister out of it and go back to your own time."

He laughed, that pained muddled type of sound that came out when a person was on the verge of losing it. "I can't. That's what I've been trying to do ever since I arrived in this gods forsaken time!" He blinked and pulled away from her, the hopelessness of the situation sinking in. He straightened to...he didn't know what. He had nowhere to go. He stood naked in the alleyway, solely adrift, his breath pulling in huge painful drafts, and barely whispered, "I can't. Not alone." He needed Toren.

"You're stuck here." Her voice softened.

He felt himself nod, unable to say the words out loud.

"Geez." She blew out a breath behind him. "That's why you're looking for Charity." Intelligent lass, she'd grasped the situation. "You knew he'd come to her. But how could you know?"

"Ah, lass. She, Charity, she told me," he answered flatly and winced at her gasp.

She came around to face him. "That can't be true. The only way you could—" She clamped her hands over her mouth again, all her hand-won color draining from her face. "No."

Col didn't say anything. She gave herself a bare moment of distress before her features hardened with resolve. Her hand clamped onto his wrist and she tugged. "You're coming with me. I want to know everything. I knew it. I knew it this morning when she took grandma's spell book. Damn it, Charity." Great, she was back to swearing even without any mobster ogres around. What a day.

Col went with her docilely. What else was he to do? He no longer had the means to help himself return home.

"Wait." He stopped suddenly, throwing the lass off-balance. Charity was going to cast a spell to return to the moment Toren appeared. Then she was going to impossibly go back to his century through the rift Toren created. 'Twas a foolhardy addle-minded thing she had done, yet she had done it all the same. Mayhap all was not lost. "How long ago?"

"What?"

"When, lass? When did my brother come?"

Chapter Ten

"That's not possible."

Lenore marched, more like dragged the shapeshifter—Col. Col Limont, ancient Guardian of Magic from the thirteen century, holy crap—to the car. Just another stroll through the alleys with a hot naked man in tow.

The few people out in this part of town gawked, but Col didn't seem to care as he rambled out his ordeal. Uninhibited or what? He stopped speaking the minute they came to the corvette and simply stood there staring. A huge smile played over his face.

Lenore folded her arms. "It's a car."

"'Tis a rare beauty of a car."

Lenore rolled her eyes. Guys and their love of chrome and leather apparently spanned across centuries. Who would have thought?

Reaching in, Lenore sorted through Gabe's gym bag and came up with long basketball shorts and a gray T-shirt. Briefs would have been nice, but hey, the guy was an ancient Scotsman so probably was accustomed to going around commando beneath his kilt anyway.

"Lenore," she told him.

He glanced up from pulling the shorts on, puzzled.

"My name. Call me Lenore, not lass."

"Oh." His lips quirked just before he drew the T-shirt over his head and climbed into the passenger seat, looking around at the interior, and nodded appreciatively. Then he was rambling again, about Charity going back through time and helping them liberate his sorcerer brother. He told her about the evil witch and the battle.

Evil witch. It was crazy. Highlander in basketball shorts. His story was a whopper, hard to believe. She didn't want to believe it. If Charity hadn't come to her this morning and told her about the visit from one Toren Limont, she wouldn't give any of this credit. It was insane.

She wanted to kick the guy to the curb and run to Charity, stop her, even while her heart went out to Col. He'd been with his family, battling a witch...and Charity had been there too. And didn't that just make her throat clamp up tight? Next thing he knows, Col is flung into a time rift and spat out to the here and now, lost, completely alone and out of his element among technology and cars and artificial lighting and just about everything. It's a miracle he made it to Oregon and was closing in on Seattle when Starch's guys scooped him up.

And the cherry to top it off: he'd missed his brother by a day.

A day.

What were the odds he'd even been spat out in time close to this time period?

"She's going to go back to the point Toren first

arrived."

Lenore hit the brakes, nearly missing a stop sign. "What?" Because *what*? "Oh no she is not. I'm ending this right now. Charity is not getting mixed up in this."

Dark brows drew down. "But it's already happened."

"Not for us. Not yet. And it's not going to happen."

"It's too late for me to go back. I've missed my chance." Pain pulled in the way he creased his brows before he smoothed his features. "But I can send a message to my family through her. They have to know what's happened."

Lenore squeezed the steering wheel. "I can't lose my sister."

The green of his eyes deepened, spearing into her soul, his own wounded soul on display. He had lost his entire family, his clan, everyone he knew...

She broke away from the intensity of his gaze. "I'm sorry. I just...I can't."

"Charity saves my brother." His voice was as soft and untouched as snow falling on a quiet night. "Without her, the witch will..." His Adam's apple bobbed.

Lenore drove through the intersection and turned onto the street leading into Charity's apartment complex, feeling like the worst kind of scum, but she would never sacrifice her sister. Not even if the entire human race depended on it.

"I'm sorry," once again she offered. "But Charity is not

going. You need to leave us alone."

Col's mouth opened to say something and the windshield shattered, exploding glass shards over them. A leathery wrinkled beast half-emerged into the car and dragged Col out onto the hood.

Chapter Eleven

Lenore slammed on the brakes, jerking the wheel, and the corvette skidded to a stop sideways across two lanes.

What were those things? No wonder Gabe called them Morlocks, holy crap. Gabe had pegged them right. Absolutely right. They were like monsters that could have stepped right out of a movie. She'd never seen anything like them. Lenore fumbled with the door and bailed out of the car, wasp and hornet spray in hand.

The beasts surrounded her, well, more to the point, Col. They were definitely after Col.

They were like troglodytes come to life, all long muscled arms, and leathery flappy skin that looked like it would slide off with the least bit of coaxing. Most alarming were the rows of small daggered teeth, like baby rats. Gray. Everything about them was different hues of gray.

Col was on his back, having been dragged to the road. Beneath those gray teeth. She aimed the spray. No, he was up, kicking one of the trogs in its slurpy stomach and rolling into another's legs and up again to his feet.

Lenore's jaw dropped at the sheer beauty of his movements as though he had an innate sense of where the creatures would be and he hit them with lethal precision.

He flung one of the beasts away and Lenore showered it with a flume of wasp spray. The thing dropped to the ground, shrieking, gouging at it eyes. Kills wasps, hornets, bees and your everyday household smelly monster. Or at least got their attention.

Stunned, the other beasts jerked their heads toward her. Low growls emitted from rubbery throats. She hadn't been a target before, but she'd just made herself one.

"Run!" Col shouted, elbowing a beastie in the jaw while another latched around his waist and took a bite.

Right. Because she was the type of girl to tuck tail and run. She sprayed two more Morlocks that came at her. It seemed to take effect, kind of, somehow penetrating those weird eye scars or maybe just throwing their other senses out of whack. Who knew? But if it worked, it worked. Blinded for sure now, or at least desensitized, Thing One and Thing Two spun and ran into each other, claws out and doing damage. Okay now, she liked that. Lenore dodged them as they swerved past, and she ran to Col. She gave a quick spurt of spray in a wide arc, afraid to get too close and disable him. He was down and bleeding beneath a handful of the monsters.

She kicked at one, sending it face-planting in the street at the same time a swollen hand clamped around her ankle and ripped her off her feet.

The back of her head bounced on the pavement and she saw stars. Funny, she always thought that was something they made up.

Stars. Blue stars, zipping like meteors above her head.

The monsters howled. The closest one stiffened, bones rattling, making a sort of sloshing sound and caved to its knees. More blue stars flew by with the same effect.

Morlocks howled, leaping away over swerving, honking cars.

What the…?

Lenore craned her head back and found the yuppie woman striding straight for them, firing her freaky wide-butt ray gun. Her two companions ran behind her, catching monsters left and right as they scurried away.

Emboldened, one of the beasts launched into the woman, taking her down. "Get him!" she screamed, swinging her gun against the malformed head.

The guys turned their weapons toward Col, taking out the monsters battling him. He tossed the last one off, ran full-bore between the men who kept firing at the beasts after him. Then he bent and scooped Lenore up and over his shoulder.

Her fuzzy head swung into his back and she grinned, loopy-happy that he hadn't run off and left her. That was twice, she thought, keeping score. Geez, she couldn't pin a thought down.

"Stop!" The blond guy pointed his gun at Col.

Finding that terribly funny, Lenore pushed a hand on

Col's shifting butt to lift herself up a bit and sprayed the wasp spray straight into Malibu Ken's face.

He went down howling. The gun clattered to the ground and Col sprinted away. Bouncing upside down, her head rioting, Lenore was going to be sick.

A blue car streamed down the street, screeching on its brakes, spinning to a stop with the odor of burning rubber.

A door banged open. "Get in!"

Dazedly, Lenore craned her face up. "Grandma?"

Chapter Twelve

It was a wild ride through the streets with Grandma's Lexus sporting new dents as trogs thudded into the car. Lenore couldn't be sure, but she thought grandma drove into a few of them.

Lenore struggled to sit upright for a better view, but Col had her pinned securely to his side in the back seat, the palm of his large hand at the back of her head.

It was...nice.

She snuggled her face into the soft folds of his gore-splattered T-shirt, pressing into the hard contours of his stomach beneath. He was hard and soft. Like a hard-shelled candy, she sighed, her thoughts floating away on a hazy river of mud. She should know that about him, his soft sweet interior she'd never guess by the rough exterior. But she knew because she'd been up close and personal inside his essence. She knew how fiercely he loved his family and how hard he fought to protect them. Which was sweet. A sweet protector. Soft and hard.

She liked that. She liked that a lot.

And he had protected her as well. He saved her twice now. She twisted to get a better look at him, her protector candy. The car flew over a bump and pain ricocheted off the back of her head, blinding her.

She must have moaned because Col's arm tightened

and his hand curled with more pressure against her head.

"What's wrong with my granddaughter?" Grandma's voice floated across the back of her seat like the liquid neon curlicues of a bar sign. Lenore squinted, wishing the words would stop dancing because she was seriously about to hurl all over Col's soft and hard lap.

"She's taken a hard clop to the head." His accent blazed a path of heat along her skin.

The tires squealed beneath them and the patch of sky behind the rear windows spun crazily. Lenore squeezed her eyes closed against the red bludgeoning in her head and fled into blackness.

She came to and felt herself cradled against a chest, where slapping footsteps echoed the rhythm of a heartbeat against the side of her face.

"Put her down here."

She had been up?

More shifting, more spikes of pain and her brain sloshed around inside her skull. Col's warmth drifted away and she keenly missed his presence. She wanted him back, felt her arms lift like a child asking to be picked up again.

An abrupt heat poured into her chest and spread through her veins, moving upward into her neck where it tingled across her scalp. Healing energy, her mind filled in vaguely. The focused pain at the back of her head drained to a dull ache and the haziness cleared.

A tap to her wrist brought her eyes open.

Her grandmother counted her pulse, gaze intent on her wrist watch.

A new kind of warmth spilled through Lenore. "Thanks, Grandma."

Judith Greves had served as a nurse in Her Majesty's Royal Navy during World War Two. She was also a healer extraordinaire, far more skilled than she or Charity could ever hope to become, though Grandma maintained that they had the gift in full, yet the quality of magic available to access from the earth had lessened with each generation.

Grandma nodded and Lenore's gaze shifted to Col. He crouched beside her, bleeding cuts and bruises darkening his face, his eyes so full of unmasked concern she thought she'd burn beneath the intensity.

"Hey," she slurred.

His eyes crinkled. "Ye dinna tell me ye were of the Highlands." Ah. He must have gathered as much from her grandma's burr.

He tugged at a strand of her hair. "I should have recognized 'twas so by yer streak of stubbornness. Yer a braw lass."

She didn't know what that meant, but felt heat creep into her cheeks.

"'Tis all well and good," Grandma clucked. "Now let's see to you, shifter."

Instantly alarmed, remembering the Morlock sinking

its baby shark teeth into Col's waist, Lenore pulled up in her seat. Or rather, the bed she was on, as apparently they were in an indescript hotel room, seaside landscape nailed to the wall and all. As though anyone would want to steal a lousy print.

Lenore took in the wet red stain coating Col's shirt and shorts. Not that ruining Gabe's ugly gym wear was a tragedy. From the moment she'd pulled Starch's tarp off of him, he'd been cut and bruised and the Morlocks had only done worse and worse to him. "You should have healed him instead."

As skilled as Grandma was, she only had so much magic in her to spare. A healer's magic replenished, but it took time.

"You believe he gave me that choice," she clucked. "He'd have none of that until I saw to you." Grandma's features softened, before going firm and dragging Col up by the arm. "But he'll do as he's told now, aye?"

Eyes widening, Col let her maneuver him to the bed complacently, hissing as he sat.

"I'll need your help, luv."

Lenore nodded, uncertain. The teeth marks were bad, torn through flesh as the little monster had been ripped from him. She'd never attempted to heal anything this bad before and what of possible infection? Who knew what kind of decay rotted on those nasty little rat teeth? They'd have to look for any infection and pull it from him before it took hold.

"'Tis really not that bad." Col attempted to get up.

Grandma was having none of that and pressed down on his shoulder to keep him in place, which, of course, was laughable with his size, but apparently he wasn't the type to fight an old woman. "This is going to hurt. Lenore?"

Lenore nodded, not all that comfortable with doing this. What if she couldn't? Her grandmother was already weakened from healing her. Who was she kidding? She was afraid of him, of falling into his essence again and this time not having the fortitude to leave him, especially after being with him while he was conscious, knowing how deeply he cared for people—how he hadn't left her to the monsters or the yuppie gang. Plus, what would Grandma think? She'd see right through whatever this was that was going on between her and the Highlander. She didn't understand it herself and she certainly wasn't ready for that kind of scrutiny.

As though reading her misgivings, Grandma clasped Lenore's hand and placed it on top of the bloodied shirt above Col's heart. "I'll guide you."

Chapter Thirteen

The pain was undeniable. Col gritted his teeth against the tide and concentrated on the two women. Their hands were heavy upon the material of his shirt, warm as their healing magic entered him.

'Twas a strange feeling. He'd endured healings before, of course. Many times. One didn't live among a clan of magic wielders, the youngest doted upon member of the four sibling guardians, without the slightest broken arm or bruised head being focused upon by one of the several healers within the village.

But this felt different, a lighter touch, feathery soft. He felt the difference in the two healers' essences. One was brisk, forceful in her attention to detail, a bit detached, a bit jaded, while the other was unsure, almost hesitant, yet determined and brimming with such a raw compassion for life and humanity 'twas staggering. She shimmered, his Lenore. The healing magic within her glowed so bright he could see it outline her slight frame like a nimbus of light. He'd never witnessed anything like it among all the Sorceress Healers. Ever.

He felt her essence inside him, while at the same time he watched her without, drawn inexplicably to everything Lenore. Her brows scrunched in a wrinkled V, concentrating hard on what she was doing. A line of perspiration slid along her pale hairline. Her shiny violet eyes stared hard at her hand, which was locked beneath her grandmother's over his own heart.

For a senseless moment, he wondered if she was somehow stealing it. His heart. Because he'd never felt so instantly connected to anyone in his entire life.

'Twas her essence, her soul.

'Twas her.

She was a rare miracle of nature.

She was the kind of lass that fate conjured only once every generation. *By the rood*, in any generation. Had circumstances been different, he'd already be seeking her father for her hand, willing to pay any bride price...He blinked, a little unnerved by the turn of his thoughts.

The tingle of magic filtered away from him along with the women's hands and Col swallowed hard at the loss of their touch. Her touch.

Her gaze flicked up to meet his, shyly beneath long lashes, and he saw it within her too, a myriad of emotions. Wonder and unease so intense his heart clenched up into a tight little painful knot. 'Twas just a flash, that emotion, before she let her eyes drop, but he'd seen it, knew that she'd been affected as much as him.

He rucked up his shirt to inspect the bite marks above his hip bone. Both women leaned in to see as well. 'Twas better, if not fully healed. The skin was tight where the creature had bitten into him, the edges raw and puckered, but closed together as though the beast had bitten him days ago instead of a short time past. 'Twould leave him an impressive scar. They hadn't done much to the other cuts and scrapes. He'd simply have to endure those longer, which in a way made him smile. The healers of his clan doted on him far too much and would never have tolerated leaving him with any wounds. He'd never been allowed to retain a scar before.

"My gratitude." He nodded to Lenore's grandmother, unable to look at the lass so reality again, not with the residue of the intimate thoughts about her swirling in his head.

If either suspected, or felt what he'd been focused upon while rooting around inside him, it wasn't apparent.

Lenore blew out a weary breath. "Grandma, how are you here?"

"Your boyfriend called me."

"Gabe? He is not my boyfriend."

"Well, he was in enough of a frazzle over you. Good thing too, luv. I was nearly to your sister's apartment when I saw those nasty creatures attacking. What are those things?"

"You don't know?" Lenore's tone was so shocked, Col couldn't help swinging his gaze to her. She clearly expected her grandmother to have recognized the hideous beats.

The older woman's eyes narrowed. She was a

handsome woman, this Judith Greves, who introduced herself to him as he carried Lenore into this strange little room. She had a regal air about her and lines at her eyes, betraying a lifetime that had known both joy and unhappiness. She wore her dark hair short with touches of gray softening the drop of bangs over intense intelligent eyes. "No." She shook her head. "In all my days I've never seen or heard of the likes of those. They're something new."

"New." Lenore's nose crinkled "A new breed of supernatural creatures. Terrific."

"I don't know exactly, but I intend to find out." Her eyes sharpened. "Now then, young man, we've much to discuss, you and I." The woman lifted her hand as though to cup his cheek, and something indefinable tempered the curl of her mouth. "Ye favor your sister."

Out of anything he'd expected her to say, that wasn't one of them. Shock stole his breath, rooted him like a dead weight to the edge of the bed. His tongue was thick, hard to form a word around. "Edeen?"

This time she did touch him. Her soft wrinkled palm was warm upon his chilled hand. "I know a great deal about your family."

Col launched off the bed, wobbling, and strode across the small space. Because how was that possible? The newly scared wound in his side pulled.

"She was my friend." She stood, a fluid moment right

behind him, causing him to flinch. He sought Lenore for confirmation, finding only a confusion matching his own. Apparently Grandma hadn't confided any of this to her before now.

Judith held a folded parchment toward him. "I've had this for seventy years. It was meant for Charity, but…" She pressed it into Col's numb fingers. "I think maybe fate meant it for you."

Fate. His forehead creased. What did this have to do with his sister? Taking a deep breath, he unfolded it. The parchment was old, creased and carried the weight of the world. 'Twas written in Gaelic by his sister's hand. He walked in small circles as he read, dropping tiny broken pieces of his heart across the floor behind his steps.

Edeen wrote of a long slumber, awakened by a vampire in the year of our Lord Nineteen Hundred Forty-One in an era of great war where machines dropped burning death from the sky.

She wrote of finding love and finding her purpose in a way only a woman writing to another woman would share, but she also warned Charity about the darkness in the world and the wrongness of it all. She warned of Aldreth capturing Shaw long ago on that day upon Crunfathy Hill and the darkness deep within Shaw's magic becoming the catalyst that destroyed the magical balance of the world.

Col's stomach roiled violently and the walls squeezed around him.

Shaw had been right all along. He must have felt the darkness inside him. Shaw knew he had to ferret the clan away into the Shadowood, take that part of the Fae's magic that never did belong to this world back to whence it came. Shaw must have known he didn't belong either when he decided to flee into the ether with the clan—yet he had returned to save his family.

And destroyed himself.

Destroyed the world.

Brutal heat coursed through Col's veins, leaving him suddenly weak and shaky.

Soft fingers curled around his arm. Violet eyes found his face beneath the lowered sweep of his hair. "Are you all right?"

How could he be all right when the brother who he fixed the rising and setting of the sun upon was branded as the destroyer of the world?

This was Shaw.

Shaw who had found him in the forest when at the age of five, Col ran off in fear at the onset of his first transformation. The change had been bad, strong, overpowering, and Col had nearly not survived it, had been too frightened, too young and without guidance from another shapeshifter to know what to do. Shaw had found him, had guided him through, cautioned him to concentrate on an animal he knew the best, but unfortunately, the first beast that came to mind was a little lynx he'd seen as he fled wildly through the forest so he became the lynx, lost his own mind to the animal enough that when Shaw threw his cloak around him as a net before he could run off, the lynx had fought back in pure animalistic instinct to escape. But Shaw wouldn't lose him, wouldn't risk letting him go. He wrestled the cloak bound lynx close to his own body, giving Col the time for his mind to catch up and remember who he was. 'Twas a dark confusing memory and to Col's horror, Shaw came out of it with deep bloodied gashes that ran below the left side of his rib cage.

And when it was over and Col poured out of the shift as himself, an exhausted panting child, Shaw held him, rocked him through the night in the woods away from the prying gazes of the clan as Col wept, afraid of ever going through another shift again.

Nor would Shaw go to the healers afterwards or let anyone else in the clan know what a disaster Col's first transformation had been.

To this day Shaw bore those scars for the sole purpose of sparing a little brother's humiliation.

Nay, Shaw could not have a darkness within him capable of destroying magic's balance. Col could no more believe that than he could believe all the stars had fallen from their perches in the night sky.

His throat column jumped and he handed Lenore the letter, relieved when her penetrating eyes lowered to the parchment.

He turned to her grandmother, his voice raw and cracked. "Where is my sister? Where's Edeen?" Seventy years. She'd have lived a lifetime without her clan. Alone. Without him or any of her brothers to protect her.

Judith looked away, bony shoulders bowing with her true age. "She's gone, Col. I'm so sorry. She's gone. A long time ago."

A cold numbness crept into the hollowed out center of his chest. A low buzzing stuffed his ears though it did little to dull the clarity of what she was saying. Each word struck with the penetration of an arrow.

"...coming back from gathering intelligence...hospital ship, the St. David off the coast of Africa...Luftwaffe planes...bombed...she and Roque, her husband...killed, with many others...ninety-six lost..."

He didn't understand half of what she was saying. Dead. Edeen couldn't be dead.

Everything closed tight in around him. The walls and the very air moved, hemming him in. Without a word, he swung open the door and walked outside, getting as far as the end of the long balcony.

He stopped, curling his fingers around the cool iron railing and stared down at the row of unmoving *carriages*, cars.

He felt her presence before Lenore's shoulder settled against his arm. She didn't say anything, not a word, just stood quiet and patient beside him.

Chapter Fourteen

It was simple really. What he had to do.

Stop Charity from going back to yesterday. If he could keep her from grabbing onto Toren's time rift, he could keep her from following him back to the thirteenth century.

Col's heart clenched.

That also meant Toren would be left to the witch's torture and most likely perish. Yet Edeen would not be caught within a magical slumber to perish seven hundred years later, nor would Shaw be captured, his magic turned and misshapen into a dark ugly thing by the witch.

And Col would not be thrown into the time rift and...his gaze slanted to the lass, who was aiding her grandmother to her feet.

He would never meet Lenore. Or ever know of her existence within this far distant future.

Grief as shattering as he felt for Edeen's passing, speared his heart with loss, graying everything at the edges, throwing him into a blind panic to grasp onto her tight, to not let the possibility of what they could have together sift away.

He was all too aware of what he would be sacrificing, knew with a surety he didn't fully comprehend that she was meant only for him and he for her.

And when he stopped Charity, when everything

returned, righted itself, back to the beginning, he would not even remember what it was that he had lost.

But his heart would know, wouldn't it?

Somehow, he believed, it would.

His heart had to know why a large chunk of it would never fill.

He knew exactly what he was sacrificing for Edeen, for Shaw, and for the world.

Hopefully for Toren as well. Col had to believe that. He and Edeen had planned a rescue before Charity plunked into their world. He had to believe they'd be successful on their own without her. Even without the healing she had performed upon his battered brother.

Toren had to live.

"I'll be alright." Judith patted her granddaughter's hand. "I'm not exactly without my own contacts among the magical wielders. I'll call in a few favors and get to the bottom of what those creatures are and where they came from. I'm not thrilled about those youngsters toting strange guns around either."

"Not to mention why all of them are bent on attacking young Col here."

Both women looked over at him. He'd like those questions answered as well.

Judith smiled tightly. "Your grandfather cut his meeting short in D.C. He's on his way. His contacts are a little higher up the official governmental chain than mine.

They may know something." She rolled her eyes. "Don't worry. We'll get to the bottom of this and keep Charity safe with us."

Lenore nodded.

"Good." Judith looked sideways at Col. "You. Watch over my granddaughters. Both of them."

Col nodded. Nothing would get past him to harm either of them.

Judith kissed Lenore's forehead. "Go to your sister and don't let her do anything rash. And you, sweetheart, don't be reckless either. I'll call you as soon as I know anything. We'll meet up at Charity's place in a few hours." She squeezed Lenore's arm.

A horn blasted outside. "There's my taxi." She handed Lenore a small ring with smaller keys on it. "Take my car."

Lenore watched the taxi pull onto the street. Grandma was unlike anything else and she was so grateful for her. Well into her nineties, she was as fit as an active sixty-year-old. Then again, as Grandma liked to remind them, if a healer can't keep herself and those she loved healthy and in tip-top form, what good was she?

She slanted a glance to Col. The lost and lonely sorrow in his eyes physically hurt. He'd lost his family, everyone he loved. As eager as she was to get to Charity and keep her sister from jumping down the rabbit's hole, she hurt for Col. One brother had gone to the dark side and his sister was a casualty of World War Two. She knew how she'd feel if she lost Charity. Which was a stark possibility if they couldn't get to her in time.

She huffed.

Time. It all boiled down to time and whether they could change whatever had already happened.

And what of Col? The moment they changed Charity's intended course of action, would he simply disappear from this time? Just vanish. Beside her one moment and gone the next as though he'd never existed? Would she even remember that he'd been here?

Or since it would never have happened…?

Her pulse sped up.

She didn't want that.

She didn't want to not know him, to never know that someone like him existed somewhere. It wasn't fair.

A shiver shook through her body and her belly cinched up tight. More than anything she didn't want to lose Col.

More than her sister?

She didn't know. She just didn't know.

She took her phone out and punched in Charity's button. Col watched her curiously.

"She's still not picking up," she explained, holding the cell tighter while she listened to Charity's recording of *leave a message after the beep*. "Char, as soon as you get this, call me back. It's important. Really important. I'm heading to your place. If you're there, don't go anywhere." She paused, chuffed a breath. "I mean *anywhere*."

Chapter Fifteen

"What are we going to do now?" Lenore's hands squeaked on the leather steering wheel. She'd just turned into Charity's apartment complex and stopped the car.

The bloated troglodytes were everywhere, mostly in shadows and between parked cars or behind the dumpsters, a few pressed flat on the roof lines. The darkening sky gave their dark flesh good camouflage. Several more were by Charity's door. They weren't doing anything, just waiting.

For them?

For Charity?

They could already have Charity for all she knew. Charity wasn't answering her phone. Dread tied knots in her stomach.

"How close can this *car* get me to that door?"

Lenore jerked a look at Col. His face was grim, jaw set and terrifying. He was going to go in after Charity, regardless of how many monsters were between him and her sister.

"You'll never make it."

He was already tugging the shirt over his head, grinning when his dark hair emerged. "Not in this form."

The temperature suddenly plummeted or maybe it was the blood draining to Lenore's toes. This was crazy, but she gripped the wheel tighter. She'd get him right to the front stoop if she had anything to do about it. "As close as you need."

A smile tugged at his features. "I suppose ye will. Ye're a spirited lass, Lenore Greves of Seattle." A shadow passed into his light eyes. "I—" He took her hand, curling her palm beneath his larger one. "I'll miss ye. I'll keenly miss ye."

The muscles around her heart constricted. Or perhaps that was her heart itself ripping in two. "But you won't." Her voice was small, the most fragile of sounds. "If this works, you'll be back in your time, never have come here, and you won't know me. I won't have even been born yet."

They both stared out the windshield at hulky shadows of monsters between them and the means to unmake the past couple of hours, which Lenore was beginning to realize she didn't want unmade at all.

Col nodded, coming to some indefinable decision. "If this moment is to be undone, then let us speak plainly." He did look at her then, forcing her to also turn to him by the sheer magnitude of his will. "There is something between us. I know ye feel it too. I do not understand it, but…"

Plainly then. He wanted the truth and since this would all be erased, what did it really matter? The past day would be a cosmic do-over. "It frightens me."

Col's lips firmed into a hard line and he nodded.

"Aye."

That he could admit his own fears about it, somehow made it better, eased a bit of her own uncertainty. "I'm scared that it's a false feeling born only of magic, yet now, I'm afraid I'll never feel it again. I'm also afraid it is real between us. Very real and powerful and something so rare and precious that very few people experience a connection like this and I'm so very afraid to lose it, that I'm just letting it go, letting you go, and that will be the worst mistake of my life." She pulled their joined hands to her heart where it beat crazily. "I know what has to be done for both of our families, but..." She shook her head. "I don't know what is the right thing to do."

His other hand cupped her cheek and slipped into her hair. "I don't know. I don't know either."

They stared hard into each other's faces. Lenore wondered if she memorized his features hard enough if she could somehow lock him into memories that in reality she'd never make.

"I—I'm sorry. I can't lose Charity."

He nodded as though he'd known that was the only choice all along and whispered gruffly.

"All right. Let's go get your sister."

His hands slid away from hers, warmth to cold air. "Get me close, and then leave. I cannot protect ye both."

"I'm not—"

"Lass." He clamped his lips tight and shook his head.

"Nay, I do not believe ye'll heed me on this. Charity is yer kin. I understand." He focused a soft puppy-dog look at her.

Geez, way to get under a girl's defensives. She was hopelessly lost to him. And honestly, if he asked her to walk away from this and leave Charity to her own devices, she would probably wouldn't have the strength to deny him, though she knew Col would never ask it.

"Give me a few moment's lead. I may be able to get by them without interference. Does that window lead to Charity's rooms?"

Lenore narrowed her eyes at the high small window of Charity's bathroom. "It's double-paned and latched from the inside."

"Have ye never heard of the Open Stone?"

Of course. Part of the Highland games where brawny Scots swung an assortment of things around from large stones, long spherical shaped hammers and even tree trunks. Throwing, always throwing. The Open Stone was a simple toss from one hand to measure who could throw their silly boulders the farthest.

She saw where he was going. "We'll need a pretty big rock." Wait. This was her grandmother's car. Judith Greves was anything but the typical conventional grandma. Leaning over Col, Lenore opened the glove compartment, her side brushing across his chest and she froze, closing her eyes tightly when he leaned closer, letting his chin rub the top of her hair. Did he just inhale? Tingles surged rapid-fire quick through her body. It took everything in her to focus on the task at hand. Oh, yeah, glove compartment. Charity. Monsters.

She searched through it and came up empty.

Okay. Not giving up, she rooted around beneath the driver's seat and...yatzhee, came up with a shiny revolver. Thank you Grandma. She checked the chamber for bullets. Fully loaded. Grandma didn't mess around.

Lenore grinned. "You want in through the window, big guy? Here's your first class ticket."

Col's forehead scrunched like he didn't have the foggiest what she was talking about. Yeah, right, gun meet ancient Highland warrior.

"Trust me."

At his nod, she melted. Just like that, he took her word that she knew what she was doing.

She hoped to hell his confidence wasn't wasted. "Ready?" She turned the engine over. Outside, the Morlocks faces swiveled toward the sound. Game on.

Col nodded again and instantly shimmered with light, a glowing pulsing nimbus outlining his form, filling the car with brightness. If the Morlocks didn't see that, they were truly blind beneath those yucky eye scarring.

Col's transformation was beautiful. He was beautiful. Like looking into his soul again only this time from the outside. She should know. She'd been inside him.

He looked like tiny bursts of light pulsing, changing in shape like a mass of glowing honeybees, forever fluctuating and shrinking.

And then he was gone. The light simply blinked out, plunging the car back into a velvet gloom.

A dragonfly hovered above the pool of Gabe's clothes that had dropped in the seat. The sneakers lay on the floorboards. Wings buzzing, the dragonfly floated toward the closed window. It was amazing that all that Col was, his huge force of spirit, could fit in such a tiny miniscule thing.

"Kay, hang on. I'm going in."

She didn't know if Col could understand her, but, he floated down and landed on the seat. Lenore had the sudden crazy thought that she should buckle him in, which was ridiculous—adrenaline hysterics?—so she checked the gun instead, hit the button to roll down the windows and took a steadying breath. Shapes moved in front of the windshield, the beasts must have noticed Col shifting after all.

Holy Geez, what was she doing?

She felt like the getaway driver-slash-bodyguard for a dragonfly. How cartoonish was that?

Lenore punched the gas, shifted into gear and the Lexus shot forward. She hit two monsters head-on, screaming at the thunk of bodies on metal as they sailed over the car. Lexus's were designed for being aerodynamic after all. One hit the windshield and bounced off, leaving spider web veins in the glass.

Lenore sped on, hitting the brakes and sliding sideways into a jeep parked in front of Charity's door.

Morlocks dropped off the buildings, swarming over both vehicles.

Twisting to the side, Lenore aimed high and blasted three shots out the passenger side window.

The window in Charity's bathroom shattered.

Don't be next to the window, Charity, don't be in the bathroom, which was why she'd aimed at a high angle, but still...

Lenore couldn't see dragonfly Col. He was too small. She wasn't sure if he'd gotten out of the car.

A monster dove into the back of the car through the broken back window. Lenore shot him in the eye. Thick gray nasty blood splattered her face, coated the leather seats. Grandma was going to love that. He dropped to the seat, half his head gone, and his entire stench present.

Another leapt onto the windshield, slamming its fist into the spider web cracks, and claws ripped into her hair from the driver's side window, scraping along her scalp, and pulling her head into the door.

Lenore did as she was told, get Col close and get out of there, excellent idea, and punched the gas, side-swiping another parked car.

Blue light whistled by. The trog using her hair as a

rope screamed, twirling away, ripping strands from her head as it fell.

Lenore jerked the wheel, tires squealing and the beast on the windshield rolled away, taking the wiper blade with it.

Hitting the brakes, the back wheels jumped a curb and she squeaked to a stop, facing the way she'd come. Smoke lifted out from the sides of the car's hood. Beasts were squeezing into Charity's broken window, one after the other, even while the three yuppies poured their strange glowing ray gun bullets into them, dropping the beasties to writhing masses of injured globs on the ground. The trogs were taking a beating, but even the yuppies' bullets weren't enough to keep them down for good. They seemed to just slow them enough and make them mad. Geez, what did it take to kill one of them?

Lenore thumped out of the car. She had a gun of her own and fired the whole of her chamber into the monsters getting closest to the window.

There were too many of them and more coming out of the shadows, massing outside of Charity's door. Where they had been content to wait outside, once Col went in, the Morlocks had gone crazy, trying to follow him. It didn't make sense. It was almost as if they knew what Charity was up to and didn't want anyone to interfere. Especially not Col. Which was completely messed up. What did monsters have to do with her sister going back into time?

What difference could it possibly make to them?

Or was it just the scent of shapeshifter that spurred them on? Who knew? Maybe shapeshifter was a delicacy.

And what did the yuppies have to do with any of it? One minute they were ready to shoot Col and the next they were helping, keeping the beasts off him.

Charity's door suddenly gave, slamming off its hinges from the combined weight and claws of the monsters. Damn, she was out of bullets. The yuppie trio fired into the creatures, blue rays zipping like fireflies, dropping the beasts to the pavement. Too bad the Morlocks didn't know how to stay down long.

Malibu Ken raced to the monster he just shot and stabbed a knife in its ear. The body flapped and flopped and then went still. Well okay then, that worked. Head shots make all the difference. Stun them then knife them. Got it.

Following after the yuppies cleared the way, Lenore raced for the apartment door.

Col and Charity were in there.

A car alarm went off. Lights from other apartments came on. Several doors opened, people spilling out, getting an eyeful of monsters and out-of-this-world ray guns. That was going to be fun for the government to explain. Wonder what they'd make of it all. Not her problem.

One of the guy yuppies ran into the apartment after

the beasts. Lenore raced in after him and a Morlock slammed down on top of her and the world bled away.

Chapter Sixteen

She awoke a few minutes later, at least it felt that way, though it had to be longer because she wasn't where she thought she was. Or hearing pulsing ray gun fire or shrill screeches of the monsters. Someone was shouting. Several someones.

"Leave him alone!" That was the yuppie woman and one of the men shouting the same thing right over the top of her. But the screaming. That was all Col.

Lenore forced her eyes open, fighting past a grogginess that wanted to keep her securely under. Her head throbbed worse as she cracked her eyelids open.

She lay on her side, cheek pressed on cold cement covered in something moist. The yuppie woman's black-clad legs were sprawled in front of her view where she sat bending forward, as she shouted, arms stretched backward where her wrists were secured to something behind her out of sight.

On the other side of the woman, a struggle was taking place. Lenore could see several of the Morlock's distended legs, bracing and scuffling as they struggled with one angry fighting naked Highlander. His screams were guttural and harsh and all too abruptly shut off. Col's legs went limp, and then he fell into view as the Morlocks dropped him and moved away.

Eyes wide in terror, Col looked like he couldn't breathe. His body was jerking, his hands at his throat, fingers curled into some sort of weird collar the Morlocks had put on him.

"It's okay." The woman tried to pull toward him. "I know it feels like its burning, but it will pass, I promise."

Lenore lifted her head to shove up and the ground spun beneath her. By the time it settled, one of the monsters was in the process of securing Col's arms to the same pipe the woman was tied to. They stretched his arms up from where he was sprawled on the floor.

Lenore stilled, avoiding placing any attention on herself. So far she had been left untethered, probably due to being unconscious and not a threat, and she wanted to keep it that way.

She waited until the Morlock moved away to join the group of ten or twelve others across the...wherever they were. It looked like some kind of industrial warehouse basement with those wooden shipping pallets stacked about and the only ambient light coming from a glowing EXIT sign above what had to be a dark door that the yuppie guy, the blond guy she'd given a face full of wasp spray, was slumped in front of, his wrists tied together over his stomach and his leg bent at an impossible angle.

Quiet and slow to not draw attention, Lenore eased up to her elbows and crawled.

Seeing what she was up to the woman bent her legs

out of the way. "Get me out of these ropes and I can help," the woman urged, eyes staring beneath strands of her long side swept fall of bangs, a trail of blood ran down the side of her face.

"Him first. I don't know if I can trust you."

She made it to Col's side. His head pressed against his stretched out arm. He was covered in gashes of the ripped-into-with-teeth-and-claws variety. He must have put up one hell of a fight before being captured.

She touched his hairy leg and he startled, lifting his head a fraction, his forehead lined in misery, liquid eyes spilling over with worry. "Lenore," he breathed out painfully. "Are ye hurt?"

"I'm fine," she lied, her gaze blurring on the line of metal encircling his neck. The flesh beneath was red. "What have they done to you?"

"It's made of gedisite," the woman supplied. "It keeps him from shifting. He already attempted twice before they got it on him." Yeah, it'd be a little hard to keep ropes on someone who could change into something small enough to slip out.

"Gedisite. Never heard of it."

"You wouldn't have."

Lenore tamped down a flash of annoyance and went to get the collar off Col. He hissed in a breath.

She couldn't find where it joined together. It was as though it had been fused on him.

"I can get that off if you'll let me."

Lenore eased up to work on the ropes at Col's wrists instead, working on the knots while watching the Morlocks huddled across the room. They seemed to be in a heated debate. "Because you've been the soul of helpfulness."

"We have been helping you. You have no idea what's going on."

"Really? And why is that?" Lenore got the rope loosened enough that Col was able to wiggle his fingers free. "Should we have stopped and listened while you were shooting at us?"

The woman's lips tightened and she tossed her bangs out of her face, though they just fell back. "We weren't trying to kill him. Just stop him."

"I find that hard to believe when your guns were throwing ogres around the room like dolls. That kind of hit would have killed him."

"Except the charges are calibrated for body mass," the girl argued. "Bigger the target, bigger the kick. It would have only stunned you guys long enough for us to collect him."

"Collect him?"

"It's not like either of you would stop running long enough to hear us out. It's imperative we stop Col."

Every muscle Lenore had clamped up, making her head ache harder. She was afraid she knew the answer. "Stop him from what?"

"From keeping Charity from traveling to the thirteen century," Col supplied "Or going in her stead. Forgive me, Lenore, I was too late. Your sister is gone."

Lenore froze, stunned. It couldn't be too late. "No. No. We have to get out of here and go back to the apartment."

Pulling up to his elbows, Col winced. "I'm sorry, Lenore. She's no longer there. I tried. The beasts held me off."

Scooting closer to the woman, Col's arms flexed, working on the woman's restraints behind her back. "What's yer name, lass?"

"Bekah."

Col finished with the woman's bonds. "Keep yer hands behind ye, Bekah. No need to tip them off until were ready to make our move. Now this collar, ye have the means to get if off me?"

"I know how, but I can't here."

Lenore's world was shattered. *Charity was gone*. She was in no mood for games. "Seems were in this together now so you best tell him how to get it off. Now."

"Cinnamon, all right. Just rub cinnamon on it and it will dissolve."

"Cinnamon. That's it?" Sometimes it took the simplest things to work.

"Trust me. It's not that easy to get where I come from."

"Ye know where to obtain this cinnamon?" Col's dark

brows pulled together.

"Yeah," Lenore assured him. "No problem."

A swell of relief passed across his features and he nodded. "Very well, Bekah, whatever our differences, we're now in this together."

"The Sifts have taken my weapons," Bekah gritted out.

Sifts? Kay, so obviously the yuppies knew more about the beasts than they did. There'd be time for grilling her later.

"They can't stay here all night," Lenore said. Or was it day now? "Surely some of them will leave if we wait them out."

"Leave?" Bekah scoffed. "They're not going to leave now that they have what they want. Him." She nudged her head toward Col, light bangs swaying with the movement. "Don't you get it? You and me, we're just food. A snack for the trip forward, but Col Limont..."

Lenore met Col's troubled gaze, while Bekah kept talking.

"Now that they have Col, I don't know what they'll do with him. I doubt they'll kill him outright, which would be a mercy. Bring him back, I suppose, as a trophy that they were able to stop the only man who could bring about their extinction... Better yet, keep the Sifts from existing at all. What they have in mind for you cannot be good. They may cut you loose, just so they can hunt you all over again, play with their food. That would be their style."

Had she heard her right? Food?

"Fein sleep, Lenore. Now," Col warned. The Sifts were looking their way. Lenore was already low to the floor so simply eased her head to Col's knee and closed her eyes. Would they notice she had moved from the spot they'd dumped her in?

Nails scraped on the cement floor. Lenore's mouth went dry, throat tight. The scream jolted her eyes open, heart pounding.

"No," Bekah hiccupped, horror coating her voice raw.

Instead of coming to them, the trogs had gone to the yuppie with a broken leg by the door, a dozen clawed hands slashing into him. Bekah screamed for them to stop, shooting up to her feet. Col grabbed her, holding her back. Within seconds the monsters had ripped through the man's stomach, pulling out organs and ropey intestines, shoving handfuls into their mouths like starving hyenas. And the guy was still screaming.

Lenore was going to be sick.

She was yanked off the floor and shoved forward, not toward the door where the Morlocks fought over scraps and torn limbs—an arm, severed at the elbow flew in the air where an acrobatic beast snatched it in his teeth—but the other direction, toward, a dark hall. Col held onto the yuppie woman by the arm though she no longer needed any prodding either as they flew down the dark hall, running as fast and far as they cold before the Sifts noticed they were gone.

Chapter Seventeen

Lenore never ran so fast. Ravenous troglodytes chowing down on a person in front of her was pretty damn motivating. And a pretty damn good reason to swear. Dammit, dammit, dammit. They ate him alive. They ATE him. Shit. They ate him.

She reached the wide door at the end of the hall first and slammed it open into gray daylight and rain. She wasn't all that sure that if it had been locked, that would have stopped her as hopped up on adrenaline and fear as she was. They ate him. It—there weren't even words to fit how awful that was. She had to get in touch with her grandfather, get his government friends involved and nuke the damn building. Holy shit. They ate him.

She ran up the watery cement stairwell and into a filthy alleyway between the backsides of close tenement buildings laced with grated balconies and iron seesaw steps going up at least eight stories and garbage melting into the street from the rain. The Sifts hadn't exactly holed up in the ritzy part of town.

They ran on and on, putting as much distance between them and the man-eaters as they could, Col and Bekah following Lenore as though she had a clue where she was going. She didn't. Just away, as far from the Morlocks as she could get. Feeding frenzy or not, they'd notice they were gone soon enough if the door slamming behind them didn't give them a clue.

Finally her energy waned, her legs felt like rubber, and she shoved a hand out to a wall, pressing her other arm across the painful stitch tearing through the muscles in her side and promptly threw up. Long tremors rode across her pitching body.

Bekah leaned over, hands on thighs, heaving in air, and Lenore lost any shred of patience she ever had. She rammed the woman back against the wall and braced her arm across her throat.

"No more games. Tell me what the hell is going on."

Glaring, Bekah shoved back but Lenore was taking none of that and pushed back.

"My sister is gone and I just watched a man be eaten alive."

Bekah eyes blazed. "He was my friend." The steam deflated her and she went flaccid beneath Lenore's arm, her voice quiet. "He was my friend."

Lenore swallowed, and eased up just a fraction. She felt Col's presence standing behind her.

"Spill it."

"Matthew. He had a name. Matthew. Get off me and I'll tell you everything. It's what we were trying to do in the first place." Rain flattened her short hair to her scalp.

Lenore let her up and glanced at Col and did a double-take. Somewhere during their flight through the alleys he'd picked up a ratty old blanket and now had it swathed around his waist and the end flipped over his shoulder like the fashionable little Scotsman he was. Good gravy, the blanket was even plaid.

Lenore nudged Bekah to get moving. She could talk as they walked because staying in one place while Morlocks/Sifts were around wasn't an option.

"Well?"

"Where to begin?" Bekah looked skyward between the buildings.

"You said these horrible monsters could be exterminated. Sifts. What are Sifts? Start there."

"How about I start with *his* brother." She stabbed a finger toward Col. "The man who made it possible for creatures such as these to exist in the first place? By destroying the balance of all magic, Shaw Limont decided the near extinction of the human race. How about I start with that?"

"Shaw?" Col shook his head. "Nay. In my time there were never creatures such as these."

"No," Bekah said. They rounded a corner and ended up in an area Lenore recognized, close to Starch's bar. "It will take nearly a millennia for dark magic to produce the Sifts, but when it finally does, it's the beginning of the end. They reproduce like maggots and eat their weight in pounds every day. The human race will become little more than cattle. You just saw that right?"

Saw it, heard it, smelled it. It was forever seared behind her eyelids. "How do you know this?"

Bekah spun back, amber eyes glinting. "I'm from the year 2083 where *that*—" She pointed back the way they'd come. "Is everyday prime time reality."

Lenore and Col stared at Bekah, stunned. Col squinted and ran a hand down his wet hair, sluicing away rain water. "Are ye sorcerers then? Ye have the power to open time rifts. Ye could send me back."

"No."

Lenore steered them out onto a main street where a few people were out, giving them a wide berth and uncertain looks beneath umbrellas. Not every day a half-naked blanket-swaddled Highland warrior steps out of an alleyway.

"No?" Col stopped in the middle of the street, arms folded over his wide glistening chest.

A car honked, splashing water onto them.

Lenore grabbed his arm, pulling him onto the sidewalk.

"So, the future gets bad, end of the human race bad," Lenore repeated, trying to make sense of it all. "Because my sister goes to the thirteenth century, making it possible for a crazy witch to capture and turn Shaw to the dark side. Magic goes out-of-whack. Endgame is that the monsters gobble up the human race. That about the gist of it?"

Bekah sloshed through a puddle. "Crude, but accurate. Yes."

Lenore didn't mean to be unfeeling, but, geez, the entire human race reduced to sheep? She didn't know whether to be snarky or run off a cliff howling. Everyone had their own coping skills. "You obviously traveled through time, so why here? Why not go all the way to the beginning and take out the witch?"

"Because we can't. We don't have the ability to travel more than a hundred years into the past."

That explained why the yuppies were here, but not why they had done their best to stop Col. It seems they were after the same goal. To stop Charity. And why the Sifts wanted to make sure Charity made it. Without Charity's involvement there was a great possibility that the Morlocks would never exist. She could live with that, she really could. She told Bekah as much.

Except Charity was already gone. Back to yesterday to catch a ride on the High Sorcerer's time rift.

"Because Charity Greves had to go. She had to."

"Why?" Lenore and Col said at the same time.

The rain lashed out harder and they ducked beneath a storefront awning. "Because..." Bekah blinked water droplets from her lashes. "Charity comes back. A few years from now. With child."

"Toren's child?" Little frown lines bracketed Col's mouth.

'Yes, your brother's son. And this man is crazy freaky intelligent. A sorcerer in his own right, the only one left and he has an understanding of magic and science beyond…" Bekah's hands dropped. "We think the Sifts are also of your family's magic, moon sifters, like your other brother Shaw. Probably created somehow from his dark tainted magic."

"Why?" Col's face hardened. "Why would you make that leap?"

"Because like a moon sifter, they too can open time rifts. Though not as far into the past as a true rift born of a sorcerer." She pressed slender fingers against her temple. "Charity Greve's son figured it out, learned how to harness the DNA, the essence from a Sift and send us back—to this time. It's our only hope."

"To stop Col from stopping Charity." Lenore rubbed the back of her throbbing head, felt the lump beneath her matted hair. "Why bother if nothing will change?"

Bekah's eyes slanted up to Col and dread bubbled within Lenore's belly. "We were just going to stop him long enough."

"You meant to talk to him first," Lenore said.

Col's eyes went hard as flint. "Why Bekah? Now that Charity is beyond my reach, what do ye have need of me for?" He sighed and lowered his head so that his chin nearly touched his chest. "Ye meant to send me on my way back to my rightful time after ye told me all of this. Ye want me to stop my brother. Ye need me to stop Shaw from being coerced by the witch."

Bekah nodded. "Yes. By whatever means you can. Yes."

Col spun away, out into the rain, his back to them. "Stop him from turning to dark magic. And if I couldn't? Couldn't stop him?"

Bekah's tone was steel. "Then you would have to kill him."

Chapter Eighteen

Col couldn't believe what he was hearing. Kill his brother? Kill Shaw? *His brother.*

Nay.

They could not ask that of him. He'd missed the opportunity to ride back on Toren's sorcerer time rift anyway. Charity had already used her little healer's spell to go back to two days in her past... *Healer's spell.*

He swung back around to face the women. Charity was not the only healer in her family.

"Can ye perform this same spell? Get me to the night Toren came?"

Lenore's face puckered. "Yes, but it won't do any good. Unlike a rift, the spell zings you back into your own body in whatever place and condition you were at then. You'll be transported back to Starch's storeroom, tied to a pipe and drugged to your gills. Sure, you'll remember everything that has happened til now, but how is that going to help when you can barely think or move? I don't think you remember how bad you were out of it. There's nothing we can do." She grimaced, pressing her hand to the back of her head. Her beautiful eyes shimmered. "I've lost her, Col. I've lost my sister."

It took two strides to go to her and wrap her in his arms. Gently he cradled the back of her head and found the roughened rise of skin. Poor brave wounded lass.

He felt her sorrow and loss. He'd lost his family as well and counted Charity as a friend. Yet she would return, with Toren's son, his nephew. That made Charity his family too. All he had left.

If the solution was lost to them, he'd vow to at least take care of Charity and her son, mayhap discover a way to root out the Sifts before they can be created and overtake humankind, from this here and this now. They were monster of this future, were they not?

He could do that. He would. With Lenore.

His heart clenched on that, the one sunny spot of this entire mess.

He was keeping her, would make her his. For he already belonged to her.

"I can get you back two days," Bekah said it so quietly, he wasn't certain he heard her correctly.

Lenore pulled back from him, staring hard at the woman of the terrible future.

Bekah swallowed, water dripping from her hair and clothes. "I can get you back. I can get us all back."

They had to find the other man. Since the Sifts had taken everything off Bekah, her weapons and the *scientific* device that would allow her to travel to an exact point in time. As long as it wasn't more than one hundred or so years beyond her own time.

It sounded like dangerous alchemy to him. She said the man—Luke—had one as well, barring he hadn't also been captured or eaten on the spot.

Col's stomach roiled. He'd seen gruesome things during his lifetime, but, *by the rood...*

These monsters had to be dealt with. One way or another.

Lenore's little box she used to talk to people out of the air was also gone, and he, well he'd come out of the shift naked as the day he was born so now all he had was an old tartan and this cursed band burning his neck. He couldn't shift, couldn't as easily protect the women.

His palms itched for the weight of a broadsword.

"How are we going to find him?" Lenore snapped, rubbing her head with more force.

"First motel in the yellow pages that begins with K. That's where he'll be, if he's still alive." Bekah pushed dripping bangs out of her eyes.

King and Castle Motel. 'Twas not too far to travel on foot, within the same rundown section of town. It took Lenore less than a moment to sidle up to the desk clerk, flutter her large luminous eyes and the boy was ready to give her any information she asked of him.

Though partly amused at how quick the male fell to

her feminine charms, Col found he was also vastly annoyed, wanting her smiles and sly glances turned only toward him. He didn't like that at all, never felt so possessive of a woman.

But Lenore wasn't any woman.

And he would soon be leaving her. Discomfort erupted in his chest, a little remorseful twitch. He did not wish to leave her. As simple as that.

They filed into the small room, following the man, Luke, toward the back window. He also looked worse for wear, though at least dry. Bekah immediately embraced him, light head to his dark, drawing back to ask him about weapons and something they referred to as a *Squid*.

What a sea creature had to do with situation he knew not.

Lenore went immediately to the little table between the beds, lifted a strange smooth rod to the side of her face and began pressing buttons on the boxy part still on the table. Her fingers tapped nervously before her face brightened. "Gabe."

Col raised his brows in understanding. Ah. 'Twas another of the talking boxes of this time. More of the strange magic of these times, though fascinating. To be able to speak with someone leagues away. Were it possible he would like to bring this magic home.

"Yes, I'm fine. He's fine, too." Lenore shook her head. "I need your help. I know. Again. You're right. Were at the

King and Castle on Mulberry. Room Eight." She paused, listening. "The 'vettes fine. Relatively. A few windows. I had to ditch it though." Col could hear the man's voice raise in pitch. His lips twitched in amusement. The white *car* thus far had been his favorite of all the steel carriages. It rumbled like a true beast, galloping quick and low to the ground.

Glancing up at him, Lenore shook her head. "I promise, it's not bad. Outside of Charity's complex, but I think my grandma called in for it to be towed. I don't know where. Um, you'll need a set of spare keys. Yes. Okay, just stop about the car already. It's insured, right?" There was more yelling. That wasn't taken well at all. "I need you to bring any kind of weapon you have." More talking spilled out. "The whole butcher's block then. And clothes... Ah, geez, Gabe. Yes, he shifted again and he's naked. I am not going there."

Lenore's gaze slid down Col's torso, then danced back up, meeting his eyes and her cheeks quickly pinked. She spun her back to him and Col grinned.

"And clothes for me and another woman as well. I'll tell you when you get here. Please just hurry. Oh, and cinnamon. As much as you have. Yeah, all right. See you in a few."

She placed the talking rod back upon the other half and sank down on the bed.

She looked frail and weary. Lowering beside her, Col

drew her against his side, pleased when she rested her head on his shoulder.

She felt right next to him as though she fit him perfectly, was molded just for him.

"Good news." Bekah stood in front of them holding out what he could only describe as a jellyfish taken from the ocean—without the long trailing tentacles. "Luke managed to get away with his Squid intact."

Lenore leaned forward, eyeing the jellyfish skeptically. "That's the time-travel device? You call it a Squid?"

"What's wrong with Squid?" Bekah eyed the bloated blob.

"Part of the time-travel device, yes," the guy spoke up behind Bekah. He had a bruise on his cheek and dark blood stains down the torn sleeve of his shirt. "Unfortunately the key ingredient is missing."

"Which is?" Col asked, fearing he already knew. He may be from centuries in the past and everything in this era was strange and confusing, but he could keep up with the workings of a conversation. Mostly. Bekah said it earlier. Toren's son melded magic with this new alchemy—science. The missing ingredient came from the monsters themselves.

"Sift DNA." Bekah folded her arms.

Col stood. He was weary and ready to let this be done. If he had to give up Lenore, better to do not prolong the heartache. For either of them. "Let us go get this Deeun-aye."

Lenore latched onto his wrist. "Easy, big guy. Gabe will be here soon. I want that thing off your neck before we do anything."

Softening, Col looked down at her, touched. She worried for him, wanted him to have the advantage of shifting while facing the beasts.

Blinking, Lenore looked away, stabbing a finger at the Squid. Upon closer inspection, it really didn't look like anything that could live in the ocean. "How exactly does that work?"

Bekah shrugged. "Ask your nephew when you meet him. I have no idea. It absorbs the Sift DNA, changes color and…we ingest it."

"Ingest it? Eat troglodyte DNA? That's disgusting." Lenore's nose wrinkled.

Bekah frowned. "Tastes worse than you can imagine."

"It's the smell and gristly texture that gets to me," Luke replied unhelpfully.

Col grinned, beginning to like this guy.

Bekah signed wearily and slunk down into the one chair in the room, flipping a leg over its arm. "But it works."

"Wait." Lenore's eyes tracked back and forth across the floor. "If this is the last one and we use it to get Col back to Toren and Charity, how do you plan on getting back to your time?"

Luke and Bekah shared a knowing glance.

"They won't be able to," Col supplied.

"We knew before we volunteered that it was a possibility we might not make it back. We were each able to bring one Squid so we had two chances to get it right and one chance to go home." A small line appeared above Bekah's nose. "Unlike a sorcerer's true rifts, with the Squid, material items can pass through. Limited, calculated weight. Clothing, a weapon, and another Squid for us each."

"And there's only one left," Luke said.

"We get one shot at this." Bekah swung her leg off the chair, stomping her feet on the carpet. "One shot. We go back to two nights ago and you, Highlander, dive into the sorcerer's rift and go find your moon sifter brother and stop him from destroying our world.

Col nodded. He'd stop Shaw, he would. But he would not kill him. His brother. Not Shaw. He would never do that.

Silence strained between them, coating the air in thick hues.

Lenore lifted the talking rod again. "I need to tell Grandma what's going on."

Chapter Nineteen

Lenore propelled herself against Gabe the moment he walked through the door, never in her life so happy to see him. He lifted two stacked pizza boxes out of the way, teetering back on crutches while she wrapped her arms around his waist.

"Yes, I know, I have that effect on people. Can't keep their hands off me."

"Shut up," she said without heat and took the pizza boxes from him and placed them on the bed. They smelled incredible. Her mouth was watering before she opened the lids.

"Pizza? Is that pizza?" Bekah practically squealed. "I loooove pizza." Guess Italian pies were a little hard to come by in frickin happy future Morlock-world. Which was a sad statement about how things had gone. Troglodytes trying to eat you aside, a person should be able to order out for a decent meal when they wanted. That was no way for the human race to suffer.

Everyone, but Gabe, dove into the pizza with gusto. Two large with the works gone in five minutes flat.

"Well hello." Gabe looked Bekah up and down, lip curling appreciatively. "I'm Gabe. Fighter of monsters." He tapped the long cast on his leg. "I saved the shapeshifter's bacon. Perhaps they filled you in?"

"No." Bekah flicked her gaze over him, sizing him up above the cheesy slice stuffed halfway inside her mouth.

Hobbling closer, he ran his free hand up the back of her short hair. "I could tell you all about it." Lenore had the feeling he would have earned more points if he'd brought more than two pizzas. Maybe thrown in some wings.

She leaned in close to his neck, speaking around a mouthful of crust. "Maybe after I've killed a few monsters of my own."

"She's way out of your league, you know that right?" Lenore shoved the last bite of her own pizza in her mouth and asked around it. "Where's the stuff?"

"I have no league." He tossed her the keys, never taking his eyes from Bekah who hadn't budged in a sort of he or she-who-moves-first-loses stare-down. "Stuff's in the car."

Lenore went out to her Prius, ready to get out of the damp clothes. Pulling the duffel bags from her trunk, she turned and ran straight into Col's chest. Geez. She hadn't heard him at all.

He took the bags from her. Always the gentleman. "Your friend, he's..."

"Full of himself? Annoying? Yeah."

Col smiled and crazy things started fluttering around in her stomach. "A little..." His face reddened and he shrugged conspicuously. "But loyal."

She smiled back. "Yeah, he is." In some ways. But in

other ways, not so much. Gabe was Gabe, as long as there were no expectations of anything lasting, he was great.

Lenore tilted her head curiously, realizing the past hurt over Gabe was no longer there, completely absent. Staring into sharp green eyes she saw a different *lasting*, a connection so right and ripe with promise, anything she'd hoped to have with Gabe or anyone else was a pale flicker buried beneath gauze.

Col was her *lasting*. She knew that with a fervency that threatened to sweep her feet out from under her. She wanted that with him.

And she was about to lose it all when he leapt into his brother's time rift.

The cold hard slap of reality crashed into her, making her head buzz beneath a droning pulsing vibration. She pressed the flat of her hand to his chest, felt firm muscle beneath smooth skin. None of this should be happening. She shouldn't have to give him up, not when she'd just found him. Less than two days. She'd known him less than two days, and yet she knew as firmly as she knew anything that she would never be the same because of him.

And the way he was going back in time now, he wouldn't just disappear from this time line. She would remember all of this. Remember him. It already hurt like hell.

Is this how Charity felt about Toren, a man she'd known barely moments? Yet her sister had risked everything to jump back in time to save him.

"What is it?" Col leaned in so very very close.

She stared and stared, memorizing every line and angle of his face, the intense green of his eyes.

His lips twitched. The vein in his jugular jumped, the duffel bags thumped to the ground, and suddenly his hands were in her hair and his mouth moving over hers.

He was sun and heather and laughter. Savage ancient strength and yielding gentleness, the crashing of ocean waves and man oh man, she must be crazy because she swore she heard the skirl of bagpipes in the distance.

Gabe lifted a brow when they came back into the room. Ruffling her hair in front of her face, Lenore started going through the duffel bags Col placed on the bed.

Gabe had brought all the knives from his butchers block as well as a few others she hadn't known he had. And a 9mm.

She picked up the heavy gun gingerly, giving Gabe a wicked grin. "Holding out on me?"

"Sugar, I'm an open book. You just never asked." He turned his predatory gaze on Bekah. "You can ask too." He spread his arms out as far as his crutches allowed. "At the same time."

Both Col and Luke gave him bland stares.

Bekah picked up some jeans and a sweater, probably cast-offs from Gabe's girlfriend-of-the-moment. "Some secrets take a deft hand to uncover." The bathroom door closed behind her.

Gabe blew out a low whistle. "I have deft hands." He smiled and turned. With Bekah out of sight, Gabe zeroed in on Col, scanning the damp blanket riding low on his hips. Gabe's lips stretched over white teeth meant to dazzle. "Barring the homeless stench of the fabric, that's a good look for you."

Col's brows shot up, disappearing beneath long overlong bangs. As comprehension settled in his features, horrified, he shifted back a step even though there was the queen-sized bed already between them.

"Gabe, stow it." Lenore handed Col a pair of Gabe's old jeans and black T-shirt.

Gabe sat down on the edge of the bed, lifting his casted leg up onto the mattress. "Dutifully stowed." He set the crutches against the side of the bed. "So, who's going to tell me what I missed?" His gaze wandered back to Col as he tugged the denim on.

Whoa. Lenore couldn't blame him for that as the denim rode up tight buttocks to slim waist.

Bekah came out of the bathroom in black jeans and a form-fitting beige top, and started finding all sorts of interesting places to hide several blades on her person. "If you're done staring at his ass, let's get this traveling circus on the road."

Col spun abruptly, noting that Gabe was, indeed, unabashedly staring at his posterior. Eyes huge, Col spun back around and hurriedly finished dressing. "Are we absolutely sure Gabe is not a supernatural being, like a Roane?"

"A Scottish merman?" Gabe frowned. "I don't see how...oh, they're highly amorous. Well, if the tail fits..." Gabe merely shrugged, but didn't look away. "They're not real too, are they?"

Col full-out smiled, deliberately not answering.

Smothering a grin, Lenore shoved the gun in the back of her damp pants. She wasn't about to give that up and took her own change of clothes into the bathroom.

When she came out, Bekah and Gabe, of all people, were applying a mixture of moistened cinnamon to the gedisite collar around Col's throat as he sat patiently on the bed.

"Is it working?" Lenore leaned over Gabe where he sat beside Col with his leg stretched out on the mattress now.

"Seems to be," Gabe answered. "So he'll be able to shift once this is off?"

Col looked at Bekah, interested in that answer as well.

"Shouldn't be a problem."

Col blew out a breath in relief while Gabe's eyes glinted with excitement. Kid in a candy store. Luke stood sentinel by the window, watching. Apparently he'd assigned himself guard duty.

Col's face tightened in a wince, whether from the burn of the gedisite or the cinnamon, she didn't ask. Could be both. "Can I help?"

"Maybe some cloth to put on his skin beneath the band."

Lenore grabbed some washcloths from the bathroom and came back to the bed. She crawled behind Col and worked the cloths up between the collar where it immediately turned a greenish brown, soaking up the residue of cinnamon and the dissolving gedisite. She felt the heat coming off him. The muscles of his back were coiled. His lips pressed thin. His hand came up and found hers, guiding her where to place the cloth.

It was working. The metal was dissolving as Gabe and Bekah rubbed the cinnamon paste against it. The harder they rubbed, the quicker it dissolved and the more rigid Col became.

"Almost got it," Gabe exclaimed. They had a good portion of it dissolved. Unfortunately it wasn't a large enough section or malleable enough to pull open.

"Get another section in the back open like that and it will come away in two pieces." Bekah handed Lenore the paper coffee cup she'd mixed the cinnamon and water in.

She went to it at his nape, rubbing the cinnamon across the offending metal with urgency. She wanted this off him now.

"Easy. It's done." Gabe held her hand back. "See."

Carefully, Bekah pulled the two brittle halves apart, freeing Col. The skin beneath puckered in angry red welts, but Col's relieved smile was brilliant.

"Care to test it?" Gabe prodded.

"No," Lenore and Bekah both scolded him.

"Yes." Col leapt off the bed, instantly burning in a myriad of shimmering lights that flickered around him, and then became him, or rather the light became the shape of a man, fluttering firefly lights that shrank and shrank until he was gone. Denim pants dropped to the floor.

He chose a panther this time, shiny and powerful with bunching muscles beneath slick black fur. It was like witnessing something so sacred there weren't words for it.

"Wow, he's beautiful," Gabe whispered, his face radiating quiet awe.

He was right.

Excruciatingly unequivocally right. Col was beautiful.

The panther glided around the bed to Lenore, pushing his head into her palm.

She'd never been so close to a lethal predator, with claws and teeth that could tear through her throat in an instant, but this was Col.

She trusted him. She knew him, knew his soul. His essence. His eyes were the same—intensely green within the midnight fur and so filled with humor and kindness, she swallowed against the emotions consuming her and smoothed her hand over his head. Soft. He was soft and so silky. A purr rumbled deep in his throat and she laughed.

"As entertaining as this is," Luke said from the window. "We going to do this or what?"

The panther growled, but went once more into a shift, disappearing in a blaze of pulsing light and vibrating energy and reappeared in all his naked glory.

"Still…beautiful," Gabe uttered.

Lenore wanted to fault him for that, she really did, but you can't fight city hall and all that.

Once again, Col pulled on his jeans and T-shirt with a rapt audience taking in every nuance of muscle playing across skin. The redness circling his throat was evident. She wondered why she thought it might not be, why going through a transformation of pure energy might heal every wound.

Lenore grabbed up a second clip for the gun and shoved it in her pocket while Col went through the assortment of blades, planting several upon himself.

It was almost hilarious when they piled into her little Prius. Two women and two large men, all armed to the teeth, blades galore and a futuristic ray gun and heavy duty 9mm between them.

Gabe whined about being left behind, but as he was the walking wounded and in no way would be able to stretch his casted leg in the overcrowded car, it was just too damn bad. See, still swearing easily. She'd have to start a swearing jar when this was over, maybe use all the coins to go on a long vacation.

Not to mention, Lenore wasn't prepared to drag Gabe into this more than he already was.

"Well, kiddies," Bekah said from the back. "Let's go bag us a Sift."

Chapter Twenty

Turned out getting troglodyte DNA was not that difficult. They found several of the uglies still trolling around Charity's apartment complex.

Bekah did the honors, snuck up between one rooting behind the large dumpsters and slit its throat to get its attention before slamming a second blade up the flaring nostril. Gross, but effective. Guess the easiest way to put down the almost un-put-down-able monsters was to get up close and personal with the slimy gray brains. And Future Girl was scary precise with a blade. Lenore grimaced at the milky gray ooze that passed for Morlock blood as Bekah and Luke drained it into the Squid. The rubbery gelatin soaked it up like a sponge, going from translucent yellow to mottled grayish brown crap. They were supposed to eat that?

All that pizza was about to come back up.

And the smell…

Garlic and curry overcooked in a stew of rotting cabbage would be more pleasant. Don't ask how she knew that. Herbal experiment gone awry. What? She read it in a book.

"Go on." Bekah handed her a broken off piece of the soggy Squid. She didn't want to touch it, let alone eat it. She'd rather face a dozen decomposing zombies. Okay, maybe an exaggeration, but eating crap was not her thing.

She took it between two fingers. It felt as bad as it looked, slime with cartilage.

Escargot, right? It was a delicacy.

Forcing the door, they piled into Charity's empty living room.

"What now?" she asked.

"Click your heels together, Dorothy, and think of home," Luke groused.

Smirking, Bekah eyed her piece of Squid with a jaundiced eye. Guess it was even worse after already having sampled it once. That so did not help. "I have the day and minute stamped in my brain. You simply focus on your sister. And brother." She glanced up at Col. "Hang onto me and enjoy the ride. Hands inside the vehicle at all times. Ready?" She lifted the brown crap to her lips. A drop of brown crud dribbled onto her lip and Lenore was ready to puke just seeing that.

"This doesn't bother you?" Lenore asked.

Bekah's lips thinned. "They ate Matthew. And many others I care about. This doesn't bother me." Placing the brown sludge between her teeth, Bekah smiled.

"Down the hatch." Plugging her nose, Lenore squeezed the Squid past her protesting lips and her gag reflex immediately kicked in, revolting against the taste. It was like the Sifts, nightmares and death, killing for pleasure, thick snot sliding down her throat. Squinting one eye, she forced it down, nauseated at the texture.

Holy geez, she needed a gallon of water to wash this down.

She bent over, holding perfectly still and trying not to hurl, hearing those around her making their own strangled grunts, holding the crap down.

Her stomach twisted. And not in a normal going-to-regurgitate way, although there was that too. It felt like being stretched apart. From the inside.

A hard rattling vibration shook through her bones, threatening to separate every molecule.

"This is it," Bekah shouted. "Hang on!"

A roaring filled her ears, stuffed her head, like standing beneath Niagara Falls—loud, rumbling through her cells.

Col's wide fingers slipped between hers, guiding her hand to clasp around Bekah's slender wrist.

Lenore thought she was going to break apart, piece by piece. Her teeth rattled in her skull.

Then it was gone.

Everything abruptly stopped.

The roaring, the sensation of pulling apart... Everything but the taste. The horrible taste in her mouth was still there.

No, that wasn't quite right. There was still noise. Loud. Like an avalanche exploding down a mountain. An external pulsation outside of herself.

And wind.

Inside Charity's apartment. Two days in their past.

She spun to face the roar, toward the small kitchen and her heart jolted.

The sorcerer's time rift was already opened and growing in size. It was huge, larger than she'd imagined a rift to be.

Her sister was stretched out on the floor, hands clamped around the wrists of the sorcerer, his long body hidden behind the counter. His long ebony hair pulled to the side in a hurricane force twisting wind. He looked so much like Col, Lenore thought at first he'd already leapt into the fray—and the thought paralyzed her.

Knowing he planned to do just that and believing it had already happened were two entirely different things.

She couldn't let him do it. There had to be another way.

"Charity!" she called though the noise snatched her cries away.

"No, let her go." Bekah caught her arm.

The wind circled harder and harder, a whipping cyclone that swept the appliances off the counters. The floor buckled beneath them, tossing them off their feet. The cabinet doors pulled from the cupboards, bending the metal hinges. Everything was being sucked up in the vacuum of the whirlwind.

Charity and Toren lifted from the floor, caught in the

whirlpool of air, clawing to hang onto each other.

Col lunged up. Now. He was ready to go now.

The couch lifted, flew across the apartment, landing across the arched doorway between living room and kitchen, groaning and buckling against the walls, baring her view of her sister and what was happening on the other side.

Lenore pulled up to her feet, swaying with the movement of the bucking, breaking building. Plaster fell from the ceiling. Upstairs neighbors were going to love that.

And *puff, puff-puff-puff*. Tiny explosions of dusty air clouded the room, dispersing little smoke in the raging wind to reveal Sifts. Another appeared. And another. Coming through their own time portals to stop them.

Startled, but not stupid, Lenore pulled the 9mm out and shot the closest in the stomach. The next bullet went in its head. Blue light whizzed past her, nailing another.

Col was suddenly there, swirling behind her, one of his blades carving a vee straight down a Morlock's head. Well, that was another way to get to the brain. Rictus gray blood sprayed the churning air like spinach spaghetti. She'd never cared for that healthy pasta anyway and wouldn't be eating it any time soon. Or ever.

Bekah revolved close, stabbed another in the chest, but it leapt up to the ceiling where Lenore shot at it. Missed when it dropped on Col, dragging him to the floor.

Again, the beasts were concentrating their effort on him.

Fury, fear, adrenaline, or all three, stroked through Lenore. Screaming, she kicked the Sift off Col, pressed the muzzle to its jaw and fired three rounds.

The guns were good for a distraction, getting lucky when they could close to any cavity in the head, but between their blades, Col and Bekah were doing some serious damage.

Blood, guts, and who knew what else splattered them. Col whipped two knives from a Sift's underbelly. She hadn't even seen him stab the thing—and grinned devilishly up at her.

"How'd they know we'd be here?" She smacked another clip into the handle of her gun.

Bekah's face was fierce. "They ate Matthew," she growled and ducked out of the way of slashing claws.

Blue light pulsed into the veiny chest and Luke laughed, enjoying the fight. The Sift spasmed and fell flat. "The Sifts eat you, they know your innermost concerns."

And Matthew would have been worried about losing the Squids they had taken off him and Bekah. "That's how they knew about your plan to come back to my time and help Col get back to his."

Luke shot several bolts into a Morlock that just didn't want to go down. A stinging blade from Col in its ear did the trick. Lenore shot the Sift pouncing over his shoulder, sending the beast smacking into the wall. He, or the bullet coming out the other side, must have hit an electrical wire behind the sheetrock because the wall started sparking, sending eerie glows through the monster's skin like sparklers.

"They have insatiable appetites." Bekah impaled another beast, ducking under a claw. She already sported bloody tears down her shoulder. "Hard to keep things a secret. Col, go now. The rift is closing."

Lenore jerked her head toward the kitchen. The sofa upended and twirled in the raging vortex.

Charity and Toren were nowhere in sight.

And now Col was leaving her too.

The beast pinned against the wall exploded in flame. Bloated skin bubbled and peeled. Fire blew outward, catching on billowing curtains and trailed down to the carpet.

Blue light zinged around them from Luke's gun.

Col gave Lenore a frantic look. "Lass, if the circumstances were..."

She grabbed his arm, the 9mm heavy in her other hand. "I know." She swallowed, fighting back emotions pounding to release. She couldn't lose him. "I know. Go." Dense smoke coated the air.

He squeezed her fingers and was gone, leaping into the haze.

The sound of the cyclone rift was drowned by the thunder of fire. Lenore's lungs constricted. The heat baked her skin. She couldn't see Col, didn't see his final jump into the rift. Just as well. She didn't want that etched in her memory. She couldn't see Bekah either. Or Luke for that matter. Or any of the Sifts.

Where was the door?

There was nothing but bright flames behind the boiling haze of smoke.

She bent low, coughing. Her lungs burned.

Puff, puff, puff. She felt the concussions of air opening up, the Sifts making their escape to who knows when. She thumped against a chair, felt around the edges, found a rounded shoulder low to the floor.

"Lenore!" Bekah's face swam in her line of sight.

"Come on." She dragged the girl up.

The hot flames bent, danced around them, pulling sideways toward...toward what? The cyclone. The rift was still open, pulling in the heat. A Sift screamed, somewhere close. Apparently all the beasts had not exited the building.

No material substance could travel through a sorcerer's rift. Could fire? Was the fire keeping the rift open? Though she'd never seen a time rift before, no one in this century head, she knew this one wasn't normal. Something was wrong.

A window shattered, giving Lenore bearings toward

where she thought the door might be. Nearly on their hands and knees, she guided Bekah, coughing and sputtering that way.

She tasted heat and ashes, scorching her airways.

They had to get out.

The door crashed open. A crouching silhouette coughed within the smoke boiling over him. Luke. "Over here." His arm was thrown up over his head.

They were going to make it...until the ceiling crashed, wedging a chunk between them and escape. Smoke poured over the plaster.

Bekah and Lenore clung to each other, low to the floor, coughing in the hungry greedy blaze.

"Nooo!" Lenore was suddenly lifted, Bekah also, prodded forward. Col's wide hands gripped around her forearm. She'd know him anywhere. He didn't make it into the rift?

"No," Bekah screamed. "You have to go."

"As soon as yer safe."

"There's no time." Bekah wrenched away. Col grabbed for her to snatch her back, but she was quick, gone, running in the wrong direction.

Stunned and more than a little half out of it, fighting for breath through ever-tightening lungs, draped in two with Col's arm keeping her upright, well, as upright as she was going to get folded over like that, she glimpsed Bekah's lithe form run into the swirling vortex and get snatched away.

She'd been right. There was no more time.

A grating whine, impossibly louder than the screeching blaze, screamed around them, vibrating across the heat.

The rift flared outward, the shuddering of air throwing Lenore and Col off their feet, then sucked inward, closing off with a giant clap like lightning, sweeping the fire away with it.

Everything went abruptly silent. Smoke clouded the air, but the fire had been snuffed out by the vacuum power of the time rift closing.

Dully, the buzz of fire alarms broke through the cotton surrounding her ears.

Col hauled her to her feet, shouting about getting out. Everything was gray with ash and smoke.

They stumbled outside. Luke caught her other arm, guiding them across the wet pavement.

It was raining again. Several people were in the parking lot, watching the fire. She wanted to tell them it was okay now, the fire was gone.

So was her sister.

They'd failed.

"Get her in the car."

Grandma?

Lenore was pulled into the backseat of her grandmother's undamaged Lexus. Of course, the windows hadn't been broken yet by running over Morlocks. They hadn't even driven the car over here yet. Grandma must have driven it over. They'd gone back in time a few days.

Lenore sat between Col and Luke, trying to make sense of what they were saying as Grandma sped through the wet streets and the colors started seeping back into reality.

"Grandma, what are you doing here?" she managed to croak out through her burned throat.

"We've got to get you off the streets," was her only answer as the car pulled into the drop-off bay of one of Seattle's finer hotels. "Inside, all of you, quick."

They spilled out of the car, coated in soot and ash, skin red and burned, hurting. Grandma would take care of that soon, Lenore knew she would.

Grandma handed the keys off to a valet attendant and hurried them inside, bypassing the check-in desk and heading across the lavish lobby to the row of shiny elevators. Grandma's heels clicked in precise cadence on the large tiles.

Once inside, the quiet purr grounded Lenore as they rode up. Col's heartbeat was a steady thump against her back as she leaned into him, his arms locked around her waist keeping her on her feet.

Grandma was tense, more than she'd ever seen her. "You have to stay in the room where no one can see you. You came back in time without a spell or a rift. You understand what that means?"

Luke grasped it. "Our other selves from this timeline are out there."

"Yes, there are now two of each of you in this time. You can't meet. Not until your other selves have completed exactly what you have just done."

Clarity slammed all the fuzziness away. "Wait." Lenore straightened. "If our other selves are out there, we—they—still have a chance to fix this."

"Oh, honey." Grandma curled her palms over Lenore's shoulders. "Two of you can't exist at the same time. It's unnatural and time will right itself. The moment you come face-to-face with yourself, time will splice you into a whole. You have to stay here in the hotel until you've achieved what needs to be done, then I'll bring your other selves here and you'll be restored."

Lenore cupped her hands around her grandmother's elbows. "But you can get to them—us— tell them—us— what they need to do."

Sorrow deepened the fine wrinkles in her grandmother's face and Lenore understood. "You already did. That's how you knew to find us when the Sifts first attacked us. Because of now. Gabe never called you, did he? Why? Why didn't you tell us more? We could have—"

Which was confusing since none of that had happened yet for Grandma.

The elevator doors whooshed open into the

177

penthouse suite.

No one moved.

"Lenore, luv." The heavy Scottish brogue deepened with Judith's emotions. "I told you…" She smiled sadly. "Will tell you exactly what you need to hear. Everything has happened the way it should." Her hand dropped from Lenore's shoulder to take Col's wrist. "You have to trust fate. Your sister Edeen taught me that. Col Limont, you aren't finished here. You and my granddaughter have much yet to do." Her hand slipped up to his heart. "I feel it here. I know it." She turned to Lenore. "So come inside the hotel suite, remain here until your other selves catch up. Please."

Grandma stepped into the suite, looking back, her posture imploring them to follow.

The three took tentative steps and a tall figure came out of an adjoining room.

"Grandpa," Lenore cried, suddenly overcome with the enormity of it all, but somehow with her grandfather being there, it would all end up okay. He always made the impossible possible. In two strides he enfolded her in his arms. "There, there, sweetheart, everything's all right. It's a trying day you've had, but all will work out, I promise." He lifted his head and nodded. "Col. Luke." He greeted them as though they already met.

Lenore pulled back, questioning.

Grandpa smiled kindly and looked back over his

shoulder where another Col, another Luke, and herself walked into the room.

"Just let it happen," Grandpa coaxed. "Don't fight it, luv."

Lenore stared at herself. She, she was the other Lenore, catching up to her future self. Everything had already happened.

A great tugging pulled her forward as though a string were attached to her stomach, though she swore she wasn't moving.

Her entire body tingled. A loud hum throbbed through her head and memory after memory—things that hadn't happened for her yet—at least to this part of her. All of it in the penthouse suite. Grandma healing her burns, easing the pain in her throat. Luke prowling the suite like a caged lion. She and Col sitting beneath the starry sky, side by side on the balcony, backs to the railing, legs drawn up, hands and arms interlocked. Making vows. Tender kisses in the rain twenty stories above the Seattle streets, her senses on fire in an altogether different manner.

The next thing Lenore knew, she was across the room, crouched on the floor, hands curled into the plush white carpeting and staring into the dearest face she'd ever known.

His palms sank into her hair. "Oh gods, Lenore," he whispered, and kissed her, pulling her to him. He was sweet and possessive, tender and warm and the kiss was so damn sexy and mind-shattering, this time she knew she heard bagpipes and smelled blossoming heather and her senses were going to explode with how badly she wanted the Highlander and if it was possible for her essence to truly crawl inside of Col, she'd dive right through his chest.

He was hers and she was Cols, their souls and essences truly joined.

"Ah peachy, they're at it again," Luke's voice was a tinny irritant miles away. "Three days sharing a suite with this lovefest. Poke me, I'm done. Our Humpty-Dumpty selves are back together again. Can I get my own suite now?"

"Leave them be," Grandpa said. "They're entitled."

"I'm entitled. We're all entitled," Luke groused. "I need a drink."

Lenore and Col pulled back, grinning, foreheads resting together. Luke was so much fun. Memories of the last few days and what a miracle it was to touch and kiss Col whenever she wanted and simply snuggle close and hold his hand while watching TV, while poor bored Luke sat around as a third wheel, tumbled through her brain.

"Welcome back," Grandma smiled.

Grandpa was tugging Luke up from where he kneeled on the floor. "About that job offer we discussed... You remember that, right?"

Luke nodded.

"Good. Just making sure all memories have settled

together. We can go over it again if you like. My department has a keen use for someone of your knowledge." Knowledge of the future. They'd talked of it at lengths. Grandpa's associates were going nuts over all the information and new technologies Luke knew.

"I got it. It's all right here." Luke tapped his head and waved her grandfather off, crossing to the mini bar in search of that drink.

Lenore looked toward the elevator doors where she had just been a moment ago. Days ago, she guessed. She shook her head. Wow. Merging with oneself was a sensation she wouldn't soon forget.

She was clean. In different clothes. Her burns healed and memories intact that still had the haziness of dreams, though she remembered going through them, going through it all.

The rain pattered across the balcony, splashing back on their bare toes where they sat side-by-side against the sliding door beneath the awning. Lenore didn't want to move, didn't want to get out of the rain or relinquish this quiet haven above the streets where it was just her and Col, no monsters, no urgent demands to run off and save the world. Just them, quiet and together. Truly together. He took her hand within his. She leaned her head against his arm and they watched the slanting rain and waited for their lives to catch up so they could start a new one.

Col stared at their joined hands, sharing her wonder

and her sorrow, even with the sorrow and fear of his own, but he reassured her. "Charity will come back and when she does, we'll be here for her. For her and her son."

Throat tight and heart breaking, Lenore nodded against his arm. He couldn't possibly know what that meant to her.

His gaze shifted to the floor, finally speaking what he most feared. It had been in both their minds. "Bekah will kill Shaw," he confessed his fear out loud.

Lifting her face to him, Lenore cupped his cheek, loving him more than she thought it was possible to love anyone, so grateful he was here with her, and hurting for him. It hurt so bad. "Trust in fate, Col. Trust in your brother. Trust Shaw."

The End

Look for the adventurous conclusion
Highland Moon Sifter coming Spring of 2013
Learn more about the Highland Sorcery novels at
cloverautrey.org

About the Author:

Clover Autrey's books have been referred to as "Romance in the Safety Zone." The pages are chock full of adventure, attraction, fantasy and love, safe enough to read with your daughter or your grandmother, yet not so sweet it will put you in a sugar coma.

Inspired by her love of Louis L'Amour heroes, Clover (yeah, that's her real name), packed up and moved to Texas where she found a real live Texan of her own. She's been there ever since where she and Pat (who else would a Clover marry but a Patrick?) listen to the coyotes howl at the trains each evening.

Clover has had a love of stories and reading for as long as she can remember, especially inventing her own. She writes the kind of stories she loves to read, high fantasy with powerful elements of romance, where the hero and heroine must each make sacrifices to gain something even stronger.

Also Available from Clover Autrey

Death and Kisses

Two little girls waited in the same spot every day in matching yellow dresses hemmed with wide white lace. Every day one of the girls tickled the baby's toes while the mother held him on her hip. The father watched like he was king of his world. Every day our school bus barreled right through them. No one noticed but me.

I looked back. Like wispy clouds they faded into nothingness.

Pressing my forehead to the seat in front of me, I let the vibrations rattle through my body. I should be driving my own car like most of the other seniors, not packed into a hot clanking bus that grinds over dead babies.

I should have my own car by now, not anything new, but mine as long as I paid the insurance and gas. We had planned on it, even gone looking, but that was before *it* happened, when my mom and I still spoke to each other. Before I started seeing ghosts.

The bus shuddered to a stop and Mr. Henry pulled the handle crank to open the door and released us. Yellow buses lined the curb, spewing teenagers out into the windy Texas morning.

The moment I stepped onto the curb, a football whizzed by inches from my nose, followed by a running, laughing Jeff Sorenson, my onetime boyfriend. My lips shaped into a splinter of a smile, but other than his ball nearly scraping off my face, he didn't acknowledge my existence. I hunched my shoulders in preparation for the long walk of shame across the high school's front lawn.

The dark-haired boy appeared right in my path. I jolted. Goose pimples prickled across my skin. *Dead boy.* I froze, willing him to go away. He looked up at me with dark, slanted eyes. He couldn't be more than nine or ten, wearing jean shorts and an overlarge stained T-shirt. *Go away. Go away.* A heavy pressure, like being crushed by water pressed in around me. A chill floated off him that soaked down deep into my bones. I took a slow step backward. He inched forward. Heart pounding, I stopped.

The ghosts up on the roof crept closer to the rain gutters, watching. Creepy as hell. Fear pulsed along the air, claws scraping cement.

I swallowed, then whispered, "What?"

The boy vanished.

I flinched back, hands clenched, fingers moist.

Steadying my heart rate, I chanced a glance up at the roof. The twenty or so ghosts were already retreating, already shifting and stretching into lazy poses that resembled sunbathers. They would still be there when school let out. They'd be there tomorrow and the next day. They were always there. Every school building was littered with spirits the same way kids swarm onto playgrounds.

I pressed a hand against my chest and lowered my

head—better to stay unnoticed and not have to meet the eyes of the other students—*the other living students*—and walked toward the glaring row of glass doors. On an impulse I looked back over my shoulder.

And wished I hadn't.

The boy had reappeared. He tiptoed across the lawn as though each blade of grass might break, his big mournful eyes tracking me. That same pressure started to build again.

Suddenly he hissed, his mouth widening large as a shark's and he rushed me, galloping on all fours like an ape. I flung my arm up and he dispersed into smoke, swirling apart as it spewed over me.

I sucked in hard painful pants and lowered my arm, checking to see if anyone was looking at me. Trying to get my churning heart rate under control, I headed inside . . . and saw the shadowmen standing in the main entranceway.

And the morning had been going so well. First the boy, now the shadowmen.

I stopped. The flow of students moved around me, a human river split by a stone, oblivious to the dark forms loitering in the long open space between the inner and outer glass doors. I sucked in a long breath.

There was more than one way into this big school.

Slipping out of the student-stream, I ran, cutting across the lawn and around the building toward the back. I was going to be late. Stupid stupid ghosts. Why did they have to hang around schools?

I hate them, hate the bone-numbing panic that takes over whenever they show. All of a sudden I can't breathe, can't move, so helpless, useless—and the tight pressure—like being dragged under water by weights.

I should have stayed in bed. It's not like I had to be the perfect student or anything, I just really needed to graduate and get out of this school. With the accident and all, I was already behind. Plus I liked to be in my seat before everyone else so I could get there unnoticed. The less attention, the better.

I frowned, watching my steps, wishing for the millionth time it didn't have to be like this.

Hustling, I rounded the corner of one of the aluminum portable classrooms and stepped off the curb onto the loading dock adjacent the band hall. A motorcycle roared past, inches away. I flailed back, arms waving in the air, and fell hard on my butt.

The motorcycle fishtailed with a screech on pavement when the driver made a tight turn to come back. Just in front of me a scuffed boot stepped off the foot pedal to hold the bike up.

"Hey, are you okay?"

"Yeah. Uh, fine." I got up fast, glancing around at how many people were still around to see how magnificently I'd been sprawled across the curb. Some Native American guy watched from across the driveway, as still as a stone except for the subtle lift and fall of his long hair in the breeze. For a moment I thought he was real until he suddenly vanished.

My mouth went dry. I swallowed. Still, it was better that a dead guy saw my humiliation than the living vultures that were my classmates. Pathetic as that was.

The rider kicked his bike up on the kickstand. "Sure you're not hurt? I didn't even see you. You just came out of nowhere."

Story of my life. I twisted around to look for grass stains on my jeans. "Yeah." I guess I was okay. Mortification couldn't kill me. I'd learned that often enough.

"You're fine back there."

Heat instantly zipped through my veins, vastly different from the coldness I'd felt all morning.

"No dirt or grass, I mean."

So embarrassing. I jerked back around and stared at the worn boots below faded jeans.

"Here, let me get that." The guy bent to pick up my backpack. Grabbing it first, I fell back on the curb again to avoid colliding into him and we both stopped—face to face.

I stared. Dark brows angled down as though the guy really did care that I might be hurt. I blinked. No one gave me any kind of concern anymore, the dead included. An unexpected warmth drifted into my belly and I didn't exactly know what to make of that. His short dark hair was windblown from his motorcycle ride. His mouth pulled down in a frown. Intense green eyes studied me and I had the vague uncomfortable feeling that he could see through my shields if he looked close enough, which kind of freaked me out.

I'd never seen him before because even though our student body is huge, a face like that would have been permanently framed and hanging in the art district of my brain.

"That one wasn't my fault." His lips reshaped into a slightly off-kilter grin. "You're really not hurt?"

"Uh . . . I don't think so," I said stupidly. Yeah, I can be really smooth.

I snatched up my backpack and hugged it to me like a barrier. He was way too close, his eyes way too . . . I don't know . . . alive.

"I'm late for class." I got up.

He straightened as well, watching me. "O . . . kay, then."

With me standing on the curb and him lower on the cement, I looked straight at his chin, at the shadow of barely-there stubble, at the little freckle below the corner of his curved lip. "Yeah. No worries. It's cool."

"Yeah, well, next time look before you step into traffic."

My gaze snapped back to his. "Traffic? Seriously?

This is the loading dock."

That lopsided grin widened and my brain went blank. I wish he'd quit looking at me. Quit talking to me. Just quit. I wasn't used to it. I rubbed my palms along my arms.

"Uh, well. Whatever. I gotta go." Stains on my butt or not, I turned and left, slowing way down so it wouldn't seem obvious that I wanted to get away. Like I really needed some guy to start talking about how the biggest outcast in school nearly got herself run over at the loading dock.

The bike's engine revved up and I looked back. Motorcycle guy was crossing into the parking lot, long legs balancing the bike as he rolled into a space.

I shook my head, frowning at how dumb I'd just been. It had been no big deal really, but I acted like a nervous freshman, not cool at all. I just wanted to be normal again, not some freaky loser who felt like running and hiding just because someone who wasn't dead actually talked to me. I hated this. Where had all my confidence gone? Oh yeah, it fled the moment ghosts began hanging around.

Before the ghosts, I might have flirted up a storm with him. I had been good at it. It would have been a notch for him to be seen with me, a girl at the sharp tip of the popularity pyramid, not the school's resident freak I'd become.

I turned away. Who was I kidding? That was another life. There was no more normal.

3903824R00107

Printed in Great Britain
by Amazon.co.uk, Ltd.,
Marston Gate.